NO
ORDINARY
BREAD

Jim Ward

AOS Publishing, 2024

Copyright © 2024

Jim Ward

ISBN: 978-1-998662-01-2

Cover Design: Meredith Lindsay

Visit AOS Publishing's website:
www.aospublishing.com

Do mo mhuintir

BOOK

I

"Already in feudal land-ownership the ownership of the earth appears as an alien power ruling over men."

Karl Marx

We waded among high grass up to our waists, flicking the swollen heads off the stems of the wild flowers with our bamboo shoots. Forever inseparable, me and Zhu.

We crept up to the brown panelled hut. Gnats, standing still in the hot air as if suspended by magic, buzzed about the vegetation at the rear. Midges formed a mist around us; it was evening.

'He's in here.'

'We shouldn't.'

'Oh, come on.'

'What if he sees us?'

'He won't.'

In my memory, Zhu was always here, since the beginning – a world without end. Zhu leaned down to peek through the slat he had broken off.

He shut one eye while spying with the other. I waited for my turn.

'What do you see?'

'Shush.'

'Do you see him?'

Zhu didn't answer. After a couple of minutes I got tired watching him watching, so I shoved him aside.

I leaned down and looked in the slot. Inside, darkness lit by flickering candle flames; two candles on a table spread with a white cloth. Then shadows moved; I saw him. He was on his knees. I was suddenly frightened. He looked like a ghost in the candlelight. He was all white and reading from an open book that lay on the table. I saw then that he was wearing a white frock and a mauve scarf. His hands were raised apart and he rocked back and forth.

'What do you see?'

'He's in a trance...saying spells.'

'Let me see.'

'Quiet. He's having supper, I think.'

'What does he eat?'

I kept watching. He bent forward and kissed the book, made sign language, then took a silver plate with a white pancake on it and a wooden goblet. He lifted these up to the ceiling, still talking to himself, more sign language. He took the pancake and broke some off. It came apart like a rice cake. Then, he lifted this up, did the same with the goblet. He then ate the pancake and drank from the cup. All the while, the two candles made shadows on the walls.

We walked back, me and Zhu. I was silent most of the way.

'This foreigner is strange.'

'All foreigners are strange,' I answered.

'What did he do?'

'You saw him.'

'But you shoved me and watched longer.'

Zhu elbowed me, laughing through gaps in his teeth:

'Did he undress?'

I pushed him away and we walked back together.

He first came in the evening, into our village. I thought then that he was tall, but now I think it must have been that he approached from the west, as the sun was burning off its last rays and his shadow made him bigger than he was.

He was European – that, we could tell; we had heard of them, those men who dressed in black.

We were playing in the street as he passed, carrying a backpack. A coolie pulled along a wagon loaded with curiosities.

We ran behind, hoping something would fall off. The dogs followed too. I watched as Zhang and Wei walked beside him for some of the way. He paid them no attention at first, but after a while he nodded at them, smiling uncomfortably.

The villagers stopped their chores as he passed each house, the women and old men. The men, those who came back from fighting the Japanese, were either away fighting again or else fishing The River. Only the sick stayed at home.

No village is the same, yet ours was no different, either. Huts sprouted everywhere on elevated ground among bamboo and broadleaf, beside the stream, which was a tributary of The River and where the women washed clothes and fetched fresh water. The main street was covered in dirt and purposefully wide. The Kuomintang insisted on western-type modernisation. Nanking ruled. I had grown up hearing of Nanking and his rules. I had no real clue who he or it was, until it would make sense in a very real way. And it was through this stranger that this would come about.

In a way, I would have learned sooner or later given the state of our country, but see, I was ten when all this happened.

We skipped and trailed along after him, holding twigs and beating the wagon until the women called after us to come inside. All mothers, except in my case, it was Li, my sister. She ran across the wide street and pulled me back by the hand.

In our home, I sat on the wooden bench at the table.

'Why did you pull me back, Li?'

'You shouldn't follow, that's why.' She took down two bowls and set them on the table. There was rice steaming in the big colander.

'But we all did.'

'We all did! If Zhu and the rest jumped into Yangzi river to drown, would you too?'

'That's different. I was curious. He's strange.'

'He's *Laowai.* Leave him alone.'

Li took the colander and ladled steaming rice into our bowls. The rice was lumpy, stuck in blobs. Then, she added dumpling   .

'Is there no meat? No fish?'

'Just eat what I've given,' she said impatiently.

'But I thought we'd have fish for supper today.'

'Be quiet.' She spooned rice into her mouth.

Li was my older sister, by seven years. She looked after me. Mother died from fever when I was very young. There was sickness back then, a lot of it. Yes, and famine. Our father went to fight the Japanese and hadn't returned. Most of the men from the village went to fight. When those that lasted came back, the Kuomintang took them to fight the Communists. We lived in fear of the Communists. We heard the stories of villages taken by the Communists and what they did there. When people went into the woods, they went in groups, and we never went into the hills anymore.

'I'm going out with Zhu later.'

'Just stay away from the *Laowai*, that's all.'

'Is he a Communist?'

'All *Laowai* are in league with them.'

'Is Tang in league with the *Laowai* then?'

'Don't speak of him!' Li spat this with food in her mouth. 'Don't let anybody hear you mention him.'

She looked up to see the latch was on the cabin door. She always frightened me this way, whenever I spoke about things that made her uneasy.

A second later, there was a knock on the door. Then another. Li swallowed the morsel she was chewing and gave me a look. It was spring and still bright outside, but who could be calling, we wondered.

Li stood up, settling her hair, and before lifting the latch, she smoothed down her smock. My heart was thumping when she opened the door.

'Li…I'm so sorry I'm late. I was talking to the others…till now.'

It was Johnny. He rushed in, touching his cap. He was carrying two bream on a line.

'I've brought you these, I promised you.'

'You're too late.' Li spoke with her arms folded across her chest.

'We've already had dinner.'

'A thousand apologies, Li.' Johnny bowed his head in what looked like mocking. 'But they took so long to catch. I was fishing for hours. I didn't want to bring you just carp.'

'And talking as well, no doubt.'

'Li, it gets so lonely out in the river for hours. I have to mix when I come ashore.' Johnny was laughing. 'I keep longing for you.' Li lifted her eyes upwards.

'All week I waited for the fish you promised me.' Li took the two bream from him. She was always vexed with Johnny.

'We'll have them tomorrow.'

She fixed the two bream to a hook on the beam over the stove.

'Will you have tea?'

Johnny took off his cap and folded it, holding onto it humbly.

'Well, if you're offering me.'

Li turned to me:

'Do you have to meet Zhu now?'

She always did this, each time Johnny called round, just when I started to enjoy listening to his talk, she asked me if I had something better to do. I didn't like it when Johnny first began calling. Li didn't seem to either. But, eventually, he wore us down, bringing gossip and fresh fish. He fished The River with his uncle by day. By night Uncle Zhang would play cards with other old men, while Johnny played mischief. Johnny's father also went to fight and hadn't returned.

'Not yet. It's still early, anyway, I haven't finished supper.'

'Go now.' She pointed to the door.

Our village lay at the foot of the hills: those cone-peaked, pine-covered hills, where it was rumoured the Communists were waiting. I had never ventured into those hills out of fear of being captured or killed. Thick with evergreens, I imagined the Communists watched us from above every day. Beyond the hills were bigger towns and cities, like Nanking, Shanghai.

Before the war, men from the village went up into the hills to hunt, but only in groups; there were wild animals in the forests.

Legend says that evil spirits dwelled in the hills for more than a thousand years. Villagers always feared going up to the hills.

At the foot of the slopes formed by the conical hills was the Yangzi, our great river. We called it simply, The River. As broad as a sea, as long as eternity, she kept us fed in fish, whelks, and crayfish.

War and conflict bring death with them, that's a given. But memories of heroic and selfless sacrifice, and of tenderness, also surface. My story takes place in one village. Similar stories happened in a thousand other villages across China. It may be that these events happened when I was ten and impressionable, absorbing my surroundings, passive instead of active, waiting for my turn to be an adult and thence active.

When you're passive, you blend into the canvas, and, like canvas, you absorb, take it in. When you do things, you are active in life's theatre. It is possible to be both, but very few of us can have awareness of both at the same time – only the few, the exceptional ones; I am not exceptional.

Maybe if I was in another age they mightn't have happened. Just maybe. But history, according to Karl Marx, isn't caused by heroic personalities (or in my case, unheroic) but by the dialectic of class struggle, always moving events forward, until finally, the proletariat takes control and we arrive at the end of history.

It may be that I can remember this because it took place when I could easily absorb the happenings. I was that age. But, I now think they stand out because they were unique. After all, our country's history has undergone changes of unimaginable magnitude since then. History has been written and re-written to suit the various sides and factions. This is one history.

At first, the *Laowai* kept to himself. Me and Zhu would sneak around the back of his hut every evening to watch him perform his supper antics. He only ever ate white pancakes and drank from the goblet. Zhu, who liked food, wondered at this:

'Why only pancakes? Why never rice?'

'That is their diet,' I told him.

The villagers left him alone and went about doing their daily business. He would walk the village, sometimes buying food, smiling through forced teeth and bowing appreciatively – vegetables, rice, some fish from the fishermen, but we never saw him eat this food, only his pancakes. He wore a broad-brimmed white hat and white coat, underneath he had on a black shirt with a stiff white collar.

In the afternoons, he carried a black, leather-bound book with him and walked down towards The River, where he spent a while walking along the bank while reading from it, his forefinger touching the open page, his lips moving like a dying fish.

Those villagers who dealt with him said he spoke in Mandarin but could pick up our local dialect quickly enough. They could tell he was educated; we had heard of these *Laowai* who dressed in black.

One morning as I lay in bed, red sunlight filtering through the blinds on the window, I heard noise: a tinny, piercing sound, tinkling outside somewhere. I quickly jumped up to look out, expecting the Communists had come. Some people were standing outside their huts to see as well. I saw others walking in the direction of this din. I rushed out, fixing on my sandals. Li was already at the door.

'What is it? Is it the Communists?'

'I don't know.'

'Let me see.' I ran onto the street.

'Be careful,' she shouted after me.

The ringing became more intense. I followed it along with some others.

'It's the *Laowai*,' said one.

'He's mad,' said another.

I wasn't surprised. I had always suspected something would happen with him. Zhu thought he was funny. The villagers thought he was crazy. I asked Li what she thought. She said nothing, the way I know now, girls often do. She worried about the Communists. Yes...and Tang.

We were led by the din to the long shack on the edge of the village nearest to The River. The *Laowai* stood outside the door. The shack was long and rectangular. The main door was on the narrow side and faced west. I saw that he had cultivated the narrow path by having garden flowers lining the small distance to the door. His own hut was at the rear.

He stood, looking tall, if I remember, wearing a white robe. Then, we saw the cause of this tinny sound – he was ringing a bell with one hand, and smiling, showing his yellow teeth. There was, to his side, a white board with both Chinese and Western writing on it. I can still recall what it said:

CHURCH OF

ST FRANCIS XAVIOUR S.J.

PARISH OF ZHAOUI

Zhaoui was *our* village and hinterland. He indicated with the other hand that we go inside. Some stood, looking curious and bemused, and wouldn't go inside, but myself and a few dozen went in. I could hear Li in my head warning me to stay away, maybe that's why I went in.

Inside, we sat cross-legged on the floor; there was a wide carpet of turquoise. I considered this luxury to be big. The only other house in the village to have such an item was Xi's – he was our village Elder. Xi was old and commanded much respect. He had been an Elder for such a long time that when the Kuomintang took over, they made him Mayor.

There were about twenty-five people sitting around, mostly out of curiosity. Some older villagers declared they wanted nothing to do with this. I spotted Johnny sitting at the back with some friends, laughing and jostling each other.

At the far end of the hut was a table spread with a white cloth and two lit candles, just as I had seen before when watching the *Laowai* eat supper. On the table was the goblet and plate, again as before. Also a silver cross standing upright, the sign of the Western religions we had often heard about in stories of conquering hoards of Western knights with a red cross emblazoned on their tunics, of wars with the great Sultans of the Arab countries, of great battles, and stories of selfless sacrifices of their monks, of great artwork made by these monks.

Then, the tinkle of a bell again; the *Laowai* walked through the centre aisle along the length of the hut towards the set table. He was ringing a miniature bell this time; a tinny rattle. In his right hand he held a heavy book.

He stood tall in front of us, lay the bell down on the table, seized the book by both hands, and began speaking in broken Mandarin:

'Good morning. My name is Olivier. Père Olivier, Père Jacques Olivier, and I am your priest. Assigned to this beautiful village, in this beloved country, by *my* Superior-General, at the behest of His Holiness in Rome.'

We all looked at each other wondering what he meant. He opened the heavy book and read first in his language, then summarised it in rough Mandarin.

'In the beginning was the Word. And the Word was with God. Well, you've all heard at some point of God. He glanced over the book:

'Is there anyone here who hasn't heard of God?'

I knew very little but was too afraid to speak up.

'God is our father in Heaven. He created everything – this Earth we live on, you, the plants and animals, the sun, which is but a star, the other stars in the skies...'

The sun is a star? On our national flag is a star – the Kuomintang's.

'Who is this Word mentioned?' He asked. His teeth looked faded yellow, in a pale, freckled face, his hair a golden colour I found fascinating. I'd never seen such colour hair.

'The Word was with God. You'll see this book' – he tapped the hard cover of the book – 'is all about the Word.

'The Word is the Son of God. There is Father, Son, AND,' he emphasised, 'Holy Ghost. Three divine persons in one God'. Consubstantial was the word he said, not in Chinese but in his own tongue, I still remember it. I practised saying it with my mouth afterwards. 'Consubstantial with each other.'

'The Word is the Son of God. Consubstantial with the Father since the beginning. In his human incarnation known as Jesus – "The Word was made flesh".' – He lifted the book high on stretched arms. I could see some of us felt frightened by this, but also enthralled.

'Jesus came amongst us, as a man, to teach us the right way, not only through very wise teachings – they're written in here.' – He tapped the book again. – 'But by example – he was sinless.'

'Born to a woman, the Virgin, who, although human herself, was conceived without Original Sin which the rest of us have – the sin of Adam and Eve, our...mankind's common ancestors – it's all here.' – He shook the book.

'But Jesus also came to offer himself in sacrifice, like a sacrificial lamb, like the unblemished lamb the ancient Jews used as a sacrifice to God. Jesus offered himself up as ransom to atone for the sin of Adam, and all our sins, yes, all the sins of humanity from the beginning to the end of the Earth, every sin, curse, and chastisement, to guarantee all of us salvation. A sinless one, condemned because he spoke truth that offended the guilty, an innocent, put to death most cruelly, because he loved us all.'

'What else did he say?' Zhu asked. 'My mother wouldn't allow me follow the bell'.

Zhu's mother was a small woman who spoke much. She often appeared fidgety.

'Does she still think the Communists watch us from up in the hills?'

'She thinks he – Père Jacques – is in league with them in some way.'

I thought about this when Zhu said it. I wanted to learn more about Père Jacques – and his book.

'He said that every week at the same time he would preach about his book – and say Mass.'

'Mass?' Zhu tried to pronounce the word 'What's that? – And what's a virgin?'

'Li, are you a virgin?'

My sister dropped the bowls into the enamel basin and jerked around to meet my eyes. What did I say?

'What do you know of these things?'

'Nothing. What things?'

Li turned away and looked down. She didn't answer. I noticed this in the nature of women when they are uncomfortable with anything, some subject or topic. They will say nothing, even if they feel a lot. Remaining silent is a tactic they often use to avoid the awkward or something to do with men. They will glance the other way, eyelids lowered, silently covering what they think, hiding truth.

A gang of women together will chatter and joke, but when a certain man passes or sits near them, they will button up or maybe just giggle among themselves.

'The *Laowai* is named Jacques. Père Jacques.'

Li nodded her head quietly, scrubbing the bowls. We had eaten boiled rice with steamed vegetables.

'He spoke of a vision, some woman.'

Li darted her head around, her eyes flaring.

'What! What did he say exactly?'

I automatically knew from this reaction that I should be careful. Like when speaking of Tang.

'He only said the man, the word, was born to the virgin.'

She stared, trying to understand what I said.

'Are you sure?'

'Yes.'

'Keep away from him. I told you to. He is not right.'

'You mean he's crazy?'

She considered this for a moment.

'Yes. That's it. He's crazy.'

And she looked away distracted, brushing back her black hair with wet hands.

And so, after reading words from a different book on the white-covered table in a tongue not his own or Chinese, he took the goblet and lifted it up high over his head, all the time facing the cross mounted on the wall, then he drank from it. Next, he lifted up a flat pancake of white, said more words, and in the same way as I had watched him before in secret, he broke some off and chewed it.

'This is Mass?' Zhu was enthralled.

'I think so.'

'What does it taste like?'

'I don't know.'

'Didn't you eat any?'

'No. He says we must prepare first. We are not yet ready. We have to confess our sins and fast before we can take it. We must be saved. But he will guide us.'

'This is some magic. That's what mother says. She won't allow me to come along.'

'Neither will Li. But I have been disobeying her the past few weeks.'

'Do you think he's a Communist spy?'

'In league with them?'

'Yes.'

I glanced around me and up into the hills. If the Communists were up there, hidden, they might be watching us right now, Zhu and me. Watching everyone in the village. Sometimes, I felt I was being watched so much by someone up there, I controlled my movements and behaviour, behaving extra normal even when there was nobody around me on the streets of our village.

I sensed eyes looking.

Springtime brings blossoms. Flowers sprout, new life appears. Animals multiply. The River in full flow seems to provide an abundance of fish than in the colder, greyer days.

Johnny kept calling round. Li greeted him more jokingly now. The tension she felt at the start was turning to familiarity, I could see.

Of course I would be told to go for a walk. I wandered through the dirt streets, my bamboo in my hand to whack the heads of weeds sprouting along the sides.

I often spied Père Jacques buying vegetables and even chicken. But I noticed he never bought certain food like birds or insects. Johnny once said he would haggle with the fishermen over certain fish.

'Here's some bream. You're lucky, I almost sold them to the *Laowai.*' Johnny laughed, throwing the fish at Li.

Li made a face but took the fish and hung them to the wooden beam.

'You won't be needing any more fish for a week,' he said.

'Why? Is the *Laowai* going to eat it all?'

Johnny laughed. 'He pays well. He haggles, but we can tell that's not his game – haggling.'

'Oh, and what's his game then? Magic?'

Johnny's face changed, then he considered out loud:

'A westerner, definitely. But no, not magic.'

'A Communist then?'

Johnny considered this.

'No. He's not Russian.'

'Neither is Mao.'

'Neither is Tang.'

Li's eyes opened wide when he said this.

'What do you mean?' she said, changing her tone of voice. I looked up from where I was sitting.

Johnny's face reddened. 'I'm sorry.' He bowed. Li turned her back, one hand holding her other arm, like she was waiting for something, to be embraced maybe. It seemed natural for a man to hold her.

Johnny changed the subject:

'No, I only meant no more fish because they will slaughter Zhan's sow tomorrow. The one he's been fattening. There will be pork, plenty of it.'

'Really?' I asked.

'Yess!' Johnny said, gripping his cap tight, seeming excited.

I jumped up.

'Did you hear, Li? Pork.'

I felt my mouth water at the prospect of crunchy pork with greasy fat dripping out of it. My belly was fed on only rice and vegetables, with whatever fish we were lucky to get from Johnny.

'You like pork?' asked Johnny, grinning.

'Ribs.' I laughed.

By day, I'd wander round the village. With the sun high, like a burning ember in both colour and intensity, the streets would be arid, clay and dust. The men were fishing The River, women swept sidewalks outside their homes. Old men sat in the shade of porches and talked. My only company when Zhu wasn't around were the village dogs.

Dogs were permitted because they barked when strangers came near. The villagers used some as hunters, after rabbit and hare in the hinterland. In hungry times dogs were eaten.

The dogs would trail behind me like I was their leader. One in particular seemed attached to me, even when I chased them all away. I nicknamed her Misha.

The General Store was owned by Mister Wu, a relation of Xi, the village mayor. Inside were all kinds of farming tools for digging and cultivating, kitchenware, and clothing for sale. I liked to sit in the shade of the awning. There, women chatted and old men sat at a table and drank tea.

I'd sit on the wooden steps leading from the entrance to the dirt street and toss tofu to Misha. She would gobble up everything, often before it hit the ground, swallowing, not ever chewing.

Even when I'd toss the food at different angles, she still managed to get her mouth to it before it fell. If it landed anywhere, it was soon devoured, along with a lot of dust. The old men were entertained by this. Misha had stronger and better fangs than they had. The old men laughed at the sight of this dog swallowing every morsel.

'That's a waste of food,' said one.

'To give it to a dog? Good tofu?'

'He's clever, the kid,' said another. 'He's getting the beast fat for the table.' Then they all laughed.

I knew in some Canton they ate dogs regularly, but the Kuomintang put a stop to this in some regions they controlled. They wanted to modernise China. I shielded the midday sun from my eyes and tried to spy into the hills – to see anything, any movement – the Communists.

'Aah,' said old Gisho. 'The sweet taste of dog.' Another grinned and nodded.

'Will we ever taste it again? Succulent dog flesh.'

I suddenly stopped feeding Misha. Misha inclined her head as if puzzled.

'When the Kuomintang leave,' said the other old man, Lu.

'How so?'

'The Communists, they will allow us to go back to eating dogs.'

'The Communists eat babies!' spoke an old woman.

'How do *you* know?'

'They attacked a village north of here and burned it to the ground. Then they cooked the babies and ate them!'

The old women covered their heads with their hands.

'Did they really?' said Lu. 'And how do you know this?'

'I was told,' the old woman said.

'And did Mao Tse Tung not say, "don't give a child a fish, but show him how to fish"?'

Just then Mister Wu came out with a sweeping brush. I could spy him earlier, looking out of his store and trying to hear the talk.

'Did he not also say, "you can't be a revolutionary if you don't eat chillies"?' said Mister Wu. 'You don't eat chillies, Lu, you only eat garlic, and I can smell your breath all the time.' Then Wu poked the women with his brush and everyone laughed.

I looked down at Misha, then squinted up into the hills, but the sun was a red disc; it blinded me.

It was a warm spring evening before sundown. I had just fetched a pail of fresh water from the stream and was slowly making my way home, Misha coming behind, when the first column of troops came on the horizon, from the same direction the priest had come a few months before. A horn-like sound, a bugle blared, then the sunburst flag carried high appeared. At first I thought it was Anti-Christ, believing all that Père Olivier had been preaching, and readied myself to run, before I saw the soldiers. Communists? But then something caused me to freeze. No, this wasn't the crimson red flag of the Communists we had all been warned of. I waited and watched as the column meandered down the hill in unison – a snakelike movement.

Led by an officer, they marched through the village with their clanking canteen bottles and loaded knapsacks, rifles and weapons jangling with the muffled sound you know can be dangerous. Villagers appeared on porches and the sidewalk to watch them enter the street. Some elders led by Mister Xi approached slowly, unsure. The column halted. The officer signalled and the men collapsed, seating themselves on the dusty street. Some had been limping. The officer saluted Mister Xi and the men, stinking of perspiration and dirt, drank from water bottles. The overly large flag, orange and blue with the star, was vivid and spectacular.

The officer and Mister Xi and his elders spoke there in the middle of the street for what seemed like ages. I watched as Mister Xi pointed in the direction of the long shack where Père Olivier had set up his church. A village boy was called over and I saw him run over to the church.

Then, as the sun crept lower and the men appeared as silhouettes on the main street, the boy returned with Père Olivier. Père Olivier's tall but hunched frame wide-stepped over. He wore his broad-brimmed hat.

They mostly kept to themselves, the Kuomintang. Occasionally they would walk through the village in their dusty uniforms. I saw the village girls stop and stand in groups watching when they passed. At first these village girls would simply stare at these soldiers like all of us, but after a while, they began to laugh and giggle. Then, once, a brave girl ran to one soldier with a little lotus flower, then ran back to her friends, laughing.

There was no Mass from Père Olivier anymore. Père Olivier's long hut was where the Kuomintang were staying – 'billeted' was the word used. Their commander was staying with Mister Xi. Mister Xi appeared pleased. He would parade proudly alongside the officer whenever he could, like he was the second-in-command.

Li did her usual daily chores – cooking and washing clothes in the stream. She seemed to be always preoccupied by some matter.

One evening before supper, as she was walking to our house carrying water, a Kuomintang casually walked up to her and he handed her a plum. Li stood still. I could see she looked puzzled at this. The soldier then tipped his kepi in salutation and she blushed. She took the plum from him without looking and hurried home.

That evening at supper – rice with sardines – she spoke little. I knew enough not to speak when Li didn't speak. She was thinking. Then before I finished she asked me if I thought uniforms looked handsome. She mentioned a few of the soldiers like she had recognised them. I, too, had noticed these. I was taken by surprise. I assumed she hadn't noticed any of them the way she went about her days, always busy.

Her days were the same: Li took two pails to the stream every morning for water. We wore smocks, tunics, and trousers. She washed and scrubbed these when needed. She went for food – to watch Li haggling at the food market was educational. She selected her purchase then showed it to the stallholder, holding it out. He would demand a price. Li pouted, shook her head, left it down. Folding her arms she threatened to walk away while still pouting. Then she smiled at the seller and said another price.

'Does Tang wear a uniform now?' I timidly asked, having considered carefully. She glared at me. I was prepared. I knew she would.

'Did you fuck him?'

I was awakened suddenly one morning. Johnny was shouting. 'That soldier?'

I came from my room as Li brushed back her hair and lay her hand on her forehead concentrating – for it was still early. She was half asleep.

'Johnny, what is the matter?'

'The soldier, the tall one. Did you fuck with him?'

'Johnny.'

'I saw him give you fruit,' said Johnny. 'I see things Li, I am not blind even though you may think I'm just a simple fisherman.'

Li reddened and did not answer, still holding her hand to her forehead.

'I bring you fresh fish every day, yet he gives you a fruit and you go with him?'

'Johnny...please, it's early.'

Johnny flung his cap about him and whacked it on the stove. He was agitated. He said again,

'Did you fuck him?'

'No, Johnny,' Li cried. But Johnny just turned and walked out.

'What's going on, Li?' I asked, still tired and sleepy.

Li looked at me. 'It's nothing,' she said 'Go back to bed, it's early'. There were tears in her eyes, I could see.

'What was wrong with Johnny, Li?'

'There's nothing wrong with Johnny,' Li said.

'But he's angry with you?'

'It is alright,' she said. 'Johnny will be alright'

'He is angry. Does he not like you anymore?'

She did not answer. Sensing something, I asked:

'Do you not like him?'

Li looked at the floor and shook her head. She sobbed gently.

'Are you in love?' I said.

Li clenched her tunic with one hand while rubbing her other hand through her dark hair. She shook her head.

'Johnny is...' she paused. 'Johnny is too *nice*,' she sobbed.

Too nice? Why was this wrong? I did not understand her.

Then the door slammed shut. We both looked out the window as Johnny marched off holding his cap as his arms swung. He had been listening.

The soldiers stood in the village main street all in orderly rows of four abreast. They carried rifles by their sides and they appeared much better than when they first came. I could not honestly put my finger on how, exactly – they just did: cleansed, no dirt, their boots blackened.

The officer walked over from Mister Xi's house; Mister Xi marched alongside him. The villagers had lined the sidewalks from early on, expecting something, regaled by this spectacle. As soon as the officer came on the street a loud noise came from the bugler's horn. Then the sunburst flag was raised by a soldier carrying it on a staff. The men on parade made some movement together and straightened up, standing as one. I watched some villagers smile and laugh at this sight, others so amazed they gasped out loud. The officer saluted the soldiers. Mister Xi saluted too, like he was part of the ceremony. Some villagers elbowed each other and said, 'now for you'.

The village girls giggled, suppressing laughter for some reason. The village youths looked on in silence. Then, as we expected the Kuomintang to march off, their officer turned to face us:

'Good people of Zhaoui,' he shouted to be heard.

'My men and I are truly humbled and grateful to you for allowing you to remain here this past week. Truly.' He bowed.

We looked at each other. An officer of this army had just bowed to us? This was big.

'I want to thank your honourable Mayor, Xi.' He turned to bow at Mister Xi, who accepted it readily.

'We appreciate your warm hospitality shown us,' he said. The girls giggled even more. 'Indeed, I believe it only fair to say...' He looked at his men. 'You are truly the greatest village in the province of Jiangsu, yes, in the whole of China.'

The villagers shuffled feet a bit at this, many blushed covering faces with hands, but all of us broke into smiles. Even Li, I noticed, smiled. Was it possible we were the greatest village?

'Mayor Xi here.' He placed a hand on Mister Xi's shoulder. 'Has told me how courageous your menfolk are.' Mister Xi licked his lips looking particularly pleased with this gratitude. He bowed and placed a hand on his breast. Some villagers cheered. A few old men appeared unhappy with this part. Mister Xi waved in the direction of the cheers.

'We...' The officer paused, then resumed. 'My men and I go now to fight the enemies of our great country, and to face whatever fates we are destined to meet.

'But, good people of Zhaoui, we also fight this foe to free us from an even greater threat than to our country. Yes, from the threat to the world even, to our planet. Our freedom is in danger – the world of commerce and enterprise. Our newly-founded Chinese Republic is threatened by Bolshevism. Our great leader, Chiang Kai-shek, has called us, who will answer?'

At the mention of 'China' the officer bowed and the men clicked their heels in unison.

'The enemy is ruthless and cunning and has plans for world domination. It will not stop in China...or Russia, they want the world! Our world – all our countries.

'Therefore,' the officer's voice softened. 'As I have agreed with Mayor Xi, if there are any of you who want to volunteer to fight with us, to fight alongside us, to fight with China, for the Republic, to fight for democracy, for freedom.' As he spoke, his second-in-command, or corporal or whatever, came forward with a notebook and began pointing to the rear of the assembled men. 'Come forward.'

The people looked around at each other.

'Don't be afraid,' the officer went on. 'Mayor Xi has approved this action.'

One, then two, boys walked forward with heads bowed. The corporal told them where to stand and noted their names. I heard him ask their age.

The officer continued speaking, mostly just repeating what he had already said, and two more youths stepped onto the street. Two very young boys then ran forward and stood in line, but quickly their mothers ran up and pulled them away.

Then I saw him, walking into the street, his cap in his hand like he was choking a fish: Johnny.

I was so surprised I inhaled a gasp. Straight away, I looked up at Li. She watched without reaction. Johnny's eyes fixed down at his feet as he too stood in line and the corporal spoke some words to him.

After about five minutes the officer stopped talking and gave a nod to the corporal. Then the bugler made a loud sound and the officer marched on, followed by the soldiers also marching in step behind the flag, followed by the corporal who led our village lads, the volunteers, behind the rest, but they did not march in step.

By now Li had gone. She had disappeared. I kept watching and saw Johnny looking behind him as he marched out, his face panning the crowd to pick out someone. But she was gone.

The remaining first days of that summer passed slowly, or so it seemed. Li carried on with her chores, so did everyone. There was no Johnny to bring fresh fish or even the fresher gossip. Though she did not talk about it, I could tell Li missed him. The other families were without their menfolk as well, those with men off fighting the war and those boys who had just joined with the Kuomintang. Families left without labour, and worrying for their safety. I often wondered, did Li worry over Johnny?

'Don't be silly!' she answered, pushing back her hair as she scrubbed a pot. I said no more then…for a while. Then said:

'Do you fear for him? At war?'

She seemed not to listen, she scrubbed the pot even harder with more effort.

At least Père Olivier had his hut back again. He carried on with Mass and ringing his bell for those to come. Without telling Li, I used to go along and memorise the strange words he used and listen to his wisdom. The crowd of followers had halved since the first days. Most people were just curious at first, more did not understand Père Olivier or his message. I used to tell Zhu all about it.

Me and Zhu went on exploring the countryside about us, with Misha now following along. We played our games. We played at war with bamboo as rifles, where we took turns at being Kuomintang and Communist. As it worked out, I was always the Communist and had to die, because Zhu insisted on being Kuomintang since his mother did not like the Communists. After a while our war games got boring; they always ended up the same – with me dead!

Once a week I went along to Père Olivier's Mass, to learn his ways and the ways of the *Laowai*. Afterwards I stayed around to assist him tidy up. Of the rest, the younger ones were gone to fight, the older ones too set in their ways. Me, I was both curious and puzzled by this religion he preached and spoke about, especially Mass. One day while tidying up I came across the flat white pancake...but it was more like a flat white bread. It was on a small silver plate. I looked to Père Olivier:

'This, Father, where shall I put this?'

Père Olivier was removing his robes, what he used to wear for Mass. 'Oh.' He looked over.

'Just leave the host to me. I'll deal with it – and don't touch it!'

I jerked my fingers back to avoid touching it. I was suddenly frightened.

'Is it dangerous to touch?'

'What? Oh, no.' He laughed. 'It's not dangerous. Just precious'

At this, he saw me look bewildered. A little piece of bread? A pancake? Precious?

'It is unleavened bread,' he went on. 'But no ordinary bread – it contains the body of our saviour.'

I studied this bread carefully to see veins, blood vessels, flesh. But all I saw was white with markings of the Christian symbol, the cross. What put that there, I thought?

'What is host?'

Père Olivier said: 'A host contains something...it hosts. In this case, it hosts Jesus.'

I looked at it again. This? I swallowed my neck. This was the Jesus he spoke about...The Word?

'Tell me more.' I was feeling excited to hear more.

Père Olivier finished disrobing and came over near me and sat down. I stared into his freckled face now becoming more sunburnt.

'For example, Jesus, in order to come into our bodies, cannot do it physically. His spirit comes into the bread, which acts as a host to be received by us as his body. It is called transubstantiation. Catholics – like me – believe this to be true.'

'Trans...' I tried to remember this word. So many strange words this past while.

'How does it taste, then?'

'You will find out soon,' he answered.

'What do you call him, anyway?'
'I call her Misha.'

'*He* is a she?' said Zhu. I nodded.

Zhu had called round and we went walking along the grassy path towards the stream.

'Misha,' he laughed.

Misha ran on ahead chasing at butterflies, rubbing her nose into dirt mounds, and generally snorting. She pissed everywhere she could. We decapitated the taller flowers in our way with bamboo sticks. A mist of midges everywhere around us as we got closer to the stream. It was a calm, mild spring evening.

Then Zhu said, 'Watch this,' and called Misha's name. When Misha paid attention, Zhu tossed the bamboo over, and Misha sprang after it. Misha returned and lay the stick at Zhu's feet, then crouched down, wanting Zhu to throw again.

'Let me,' I said, and I then threw it. Misha returned with the stick, but this time when I grabbed to throw a second time, Misha gripped the stick between her sharp teeth and a tug-of-war began with me.

Zhu laughed. 'She wants to be top dog!'

Later we sat on the bank tossing pebbles into the stream. Zhu said, while he studied Misha rolling around in mud and filth,

'What do they taste like? Dogs?'

'I don't know,' I said, horrified at the thought.

'They are a delicacy in some Canton.'

'I know. But who could do that? I mean, how could you?' I looked with fondness at Misha.

'But you eat pork,' Zhu said, 'and I like pigs. So?'

I could not answer him.

'Dogs taste nicer than pork,' Zhu went on. 'I know because my mother comes from a dog-eating region.'

'You ate a dog?' I thought of pork ribs then.

Zhu did not answer; instead he asked:

'Are you being fed fish now?'

'Lots,' I laughed.

'I hear old Zhang is cranky.'

'Sort of,' I said. 'He doesn't like mistakes...or women, it seems,' I added.

If Li had said I was being silly to ask her if she missed Johnny, there was one man in the village who most definitely missed him:

his uncle Zhang. He needed Johnny to fish with him, and as everyone knew, to cook for him. And we all knew Johnny would carry the old man home when he would spend the nights playing cards and drinking rice wine with the other old men.

I had asked Li, 'Do you miss the fish Johnny brings as much as I do?'

Li chewed, then swallowed her rice, staring blankly at me.

'I think we can eat well again, Li,' I said.

She cleared her throat. 'What do you mean?'

'It's Johnny's uncle. Zhang-ze. He needs a new helper. He asked me.'

'When? When did he ask you?'

'Today.'

'To do what?'

'Fish.'

'That's all? To fish? Not to bring him home late when he's drunk?'

'He never mentioned that to me. Only that he wants someone good and Johnny spoke highly of me.'

Li looked at me with suspicion. 'And what else did Johnny say?'

'That's all Zhang told me,' I said.

Li placed her elbows on the table, clasped her hands to her face, and considered this.

'When do you start?

'In the morning.'

'Bring home bream,' she said.

'You got the nets?' Lao said.

'I have,' said Uncle Zhang.

'Bait?' Zhang gave him a who-do-you-think-I-am look, then suddenly grabbed me and pointed me toward Lao. 'Here's the bait.' He then shook me and they both laughed.

Uncle Zhang never shaved his face. Still, to my surprise, he never grew a beard. Grey roots of stubble sprouted from his cheeks in an irregular pattern and from his ears, which stuck out from under the cap he never removed.

The day always started with Lao asking,

'You got the nets?'

'I have,' Uncle Zhang would say.

'Bait?'

'You're the bait,' Zhang said to Lao.

'It is fish we're after, not women,' laughed Lao.

'Women.' Uncle Zhang spat in the river.

'Time you got one, Zhang,' said Lao.

Uncle Zhang spat again.

'Johnny will get you one.'

Then they looked over to me and went silent.

We fished from skiffs called sampan. They had a long tall punt for moving the craft along, and some had a mast and sail – Zhang's did. We avoided colliding with the odd Junk that used The Great River for trade although the war put a stop to most of these. River Pirates too were meant to be operating upstream. Stories of many warlords, separate from the war itself, controlling much of China were plenty. Me and Zhu talked of running away and joining the gangs, even becoming warlords ourselves when we grew up.

Out on the river in the blazing midday sun, I first sweat like I was being cooked. On flat shimmering water, the sun beams down and fries you.

We threw nets over the side and dragged them along from the skiff. We also cast tall bamboo rods with many hooks on the lines and fixed them in places on deck; a bit of everything. This was fishing The River and Uncle Zhang was a master at it. The best. His hands looked like leather; brown, rough, and calloused. He always spoke of the ancient philosopher Lao Tzu like the other old people spoke of Confucius, only he seemed to know more about him than the rest, at least he had the quotes. I do not know if it was all made up or not. Lao Tzu must have had something to say about every single thing, according to Uncle Zhang. Much wisdom.

'Choose a job you love and you will never have to work a day in your life – Confucius has said,' he told me this the first day. 'That's why I fish The River still, and have done for fifty years!'

Then, *'"When you are content to be simply yourself and don't compare or compete, everyone will respect you,"* Lao says.'

I looked with much admiration at him, then at Lao.

'Did Lao really say that?' I asked.

'Not me,' said Lao laughing. 'He means Lao Tzu, an ancient Chinese – ancient like himself!' Then Zhang said:

'Curse or no curse I've fished The River.'

'Curse?' I said after him.

'Never mind old Zhang,' said Lao, listening. 'He believes he is cursed'

'Women,' spat Zhang. 'That's my curse'

'But you have no women,' laughed Lao.

'Bah!' said Zhang. 'It's a long story. What do you know about it, anyway? I don't talk. Now let's get to work,' he said, spitting, this time on his hands.

'**A**hoy, leave some fish for real men, old Zhang. I can see your crew is getting younger. Or is it you getting old?'

Zhang spat overboard. 'Lao Tzu says. "*Care about what other people think and you will always be their prisoner.*'" he roared after the other sampan. Lao smiled broadly at me and asked me, 'Do you know him?'

'No' I replied.

'It's old Zhou. He comes from Huhji. He's their champion fisherman.'

Huhji was the village a couple of kilometres up river. There was no land route to there, only by water.

The River in early summer was truly magnificent. Insects hovered over its still surface, fish surfaced to catch them so that you could almost reach out and grab them with your hand, it seemed like. But I tried and couldn't. The sun shone and glittered off the water's surface, causing us to burn. Everything was reflected in that still water like it was a sheet of glass or mirror, and so calm.

The work was hard but occasionally we would take it easy. Lao would puff his cigarettes while old Zhang and I sat there looking around us, taking it all in. The heat was stifling in those early days of summer. Once, though, Zhang piped up:

'I don't believe this will be a good summer at all.' Me and Lao laughed this off as him being silly.

Sometimes when upriver, if you stare for five minutes at one place, you will see a junk with its spiked sail, or some sampan come along.

One time, drumbeats sounded, and we looked up, alert. Something approached – ribbed sails. It was a huge junk. Five men jumped off of it to the bank and the junk struck sail. These men had towlines around their waists. They ran ahead of the junk, jerking the lines like ponies in a trap, towing the junk upriver against the current.

'That's how it's done,' said Zhang. 'They are called trackers,' he said.

They strained forward, leaning, pulling the long junk upstream. They jumped up on whatever rocks or boulders were in their way, scampering and dropping down, pulling and climbing at the same time until the junk was back with the wind or current and they could hoist the sail again. The thing that most frightened me was the lashing of the whips on their backs by an overseer of sorts whenever they slacked. I prayed I should never have to become one of these men. Yet they kept singing some song or chant as they laboured.

One evening as we docked the skiff at the village wharf after a day's hard work, Zhu was waiting there for me with Misha.

Then, a sound of the ground being pounded: circles of dirt and dust appeared over the hilltop leading to the village. A horse and rider came into our view, galloping at speed. Once again I feared the Communists – we had heard the sounds of artillery and cannon in the distance much clearer now these past few evenings, and we feared imminent invasion. However, village life went on as normal.

The people stopped as the rider came to a halt in the river street. He dismounted and said out loud:

'Who is mayor here?'

I could see he wore the uniform of the Kuomintang, the same as the regiment that had stayed with us.

Mister Xi was hurried onto the street, placing his cap on his head as he walked. He saluted the rider who spoke some words to Xi then handed him a sack. The rider bowed at Mister Xi, then mounted, and with a couple of lashes to the Mongolian pony, he rode on again.

Mister Xi then spoke:

'I bear letters here from those who are at the front fighting in the great fight for our nation. These are for the following families...'

Xi then named names and some people advanced and took their letter with a cautious bow to Xi. The last name was Zhang-ze's. The old man walked forward and received his small piece of paper.

Zhang walked back holding his letter. He held it clumsily, looking bewildered.

The next morning I went to the skiff for a day's work only to see old Zhang sitting at the wharf's end, his feet dangling over the water. He heard me come up behind.

'Who will read these to me?' he asked, showing me papers in his grip. They were Johnny's letters, I could see. Old Zhang looked up at me with sad eyes and blubbery lips.

'It feels like I have a box of gold but cannot open it.'

None of the older people in our village could read or write. Indeed, this was the case in most villages across China. Now Mister Xi could, as could his relation Wu, who owned the general store. The younger ones like Johnny had learned some school and could. Myself and Zhu, too, but only elementary. For women in China then, things were different. Girls didn't normally read or write, but Li was an exception – she wanted to learn to read and write...and did, but she pretended she couldn't. Knowledge could be dangerous, especially in women.

I could not answer Zhang.

'You know who can.' Lao elbowed me, pulling my ear to his lips and speaking lowly.

'That priest.'

I considered whether to say this to old Zhang, but my thoughts were for Johnny.

'Zhang,' I spoke softly, as if it were becoming contagious to speak soft and low. 'I know one who will be able to read these.'

He studied my face the way he did. He may not be able to read letters, but old Zhang could read faces...and people.

'Who?'

'The *Laowai*.'

'Bah!' he replied. 'Not him.'

I looked at Lao.

'But he can read. And he will keep quiet.'

This remark seemed to catch old Zhang. I knew how well Johnny liked to gossip, and it must have come from somewhere.

'Keep quiet?'

'Yes. I mean he will tell no one what is in the letters.'

Zhang rubbed his chin, considering this.

'Yes,' I said. 'He knows no one and speaks no gossip.'

'Those who know do not speak. Those who speak do not know.'

I looked quizzically at old Zhang.

'It's Lao Tzu,' he said. '*"Those who know do not speak. Those who speak do not know."*'Ha!'

Then he asked:

'What do you know of him? This *Laowai*?'

'I used to help...to watch him. And to learn.'

Zhang appeared curious. 'And did you? Learn?'

I simply shrugged.

Zhang laughed and spat.

'You and all the other old women who go to him.'

'Men go, too,' I said.

He regarded me leeringly then, like a drunk.

'Bah!' said Uncle Zhang. 'Old women of both sexes then!'

But old Zhang was not drunk when he said this, not then.

Père Olivier reached in his pocket and took out and inserted reading glasses on his beaky nose. He firstly read the letter quietly to himself, then aloud. Then he read aloud, slowly trying to understand then pronounce Johnny's words for Zhang.

Dear Uncle,

We marched for over a week, stopping in villages on the way to arrive in [BLANKED OUT].

There we discovered burnt-out settlements. Burned by Communists. Communists say they liberate those villages loyal to them and burn others.

After we cross the river [BLANKED OUT]. I saw combat for the first time. Our glorious army have a line of defence over the river. The Communists attacked us at dawn.

The sound of artillery in the distance all the time, incessantly, day and night, is really frightening. We lay behind banks on one side of the river and I was told to grab a rifle when someone got hit. Once the shooting started it seemed like an eternity, the whizz of bullets past and over us, some landing in the mounds of dirt with a thud and splash. The soldier right beside me seemed to suddenly fall asleep. I noticed blood coming from his ears. He had been shot dead beside me. I gripped his rifle as I was told to. It weighed heavy and felt so long and awkward.

I watched the others, how they fired it. So I waited. My heart was pounding. I felt breathless as bullets flew by like mosquitoes. I jerked myself up over the mound, pointed my gun at nobody, and let out a shot. It blew me backwards. I slumped down again straight away. My armpit ached. But I had fired my first shot at the enemy.

After he had read this to Zhang, Père Olivier took off his glasses and said we should pray for Johnny. He took out of his pocket beads – those beads he used to finger and mumble with. Uncle Zhang's eyes looked moist and sentimental. I had never seen this before in him, but then I did not know him very long. When Père Olivier spoke about praying he seemed to recover quickly.

'Bah! No need for your prayer. We need education, not prayers. As Lao Tzu believed.'

'Oh, we believe in education, too,' Père Olivier said.

'Bah!' Zhang waved him away.

'I...we will pray for Johnny,' Père Olivier told him.

As I walked off with Père Olivier, old Zhang said to me:

'Remember boy...Lao Tzu ...'*Those who know do not speak. Those who speak do not know.*' He tapped his finger against his nose and winked. On my way home I asked Père Olivier if that meant what I thought it meant.

'I should certainly think so,' he answered. 'But I think your sister ought to know something,' he added as I left him.

Each night that I came home from fishing the river with Uncle Zhan I would be so tired. I would slump in the easy chair, bones weary, hands becoming blistered from pulling and handling heavy, wet nets.

Li was cooking supper:

'Go wash,' she would say. 'You smell like you slept with fish.'

'What type of fish?' I asked. 'Carp or bream?'

'Sea snake,' she said, handing me a bucket and brush. Supper and indeed all our meals were good then. I had fish to bring home; we ate well.

Too tired to meet or play with Zhu, I would sleep in the chair by the fire. Around midnight I'd wake up and go to my bed.

Then, one night as I went to bed, I thought I heard a noise outside like a shuffling at the window. Frightened, I went to call Li. Her room was empty, her bed unslept in. Feeling even more frightened now, I went to the window and peeked out the curtains. Nothing, nothing there. I saw that the door was not locked, so I gently opened the latch and looked outside. Still nothing. Yet I was so sure I heard the noise, and where was Li? I went slowly outside, saw nobody, the only sounds the clicking of cicadas in a sticky night. On my way back inside I looked at the ground. I bent to pick it up. It was a cigarette, only half smoked. I examined it closely, a 'Tiger'. *'Tiger Brand Cigarettes'* was written on its band.

Puzzled and still scared, I went inside and bolted the door. I must have fallen asleep again, for around midnight I was awakened again. Knocks on the window. I panicked, leapt up to the locked door and said, 'Who's there?'

'It's me, silly, open up.' Li's voice.

Expecting Li to be angry at me for locking her out, she was instead in good spirits. She appeared to be embarrassed slightly. She seemed to be in a trance, I first thought.

'Li, where were you?'

Then she adjusted to being Li. 'Out. Don't ask questions'

'I was scared.'

'Of what?'

'Li, I thought I saw somebody.'

'Who?' she asked, she seemed startled from her bliss.

'Li, there was a noise.'

Li rushed to the door to look outside.

'There is nobody there.'

'I know.'

She looked carefully at me for a second, biting her lips.

'This *Laowai*, does he talk to you of spirits?' she asked me.

'I don't know.' I shook my head, feeling confused.

'Oh, come on, I know you see him, everyone knows. You help him.'

'Yes,' I thought. 'He says there are spirits...holy spirits and evil ones he calls demons.'

'Listen to me,' Li said, stooping down and laying her hands on my shoulders. She looked into my eyes.

'Listen...there's nothing out there in the dark that isn't there when it's light.'

'I found this,' I said, holding out the half-smoked cigarette butt. Li held it, looked serious at it, reading the brand name. She put it to her nose to smell. Then she went to the window and the door, clutching the cigarette to her breast. It was as if she had just received a letter.

For the weeks I worked The River with Old Zhang I came home exhausted every evening, slept after supper. Each time I woke up to go to my bed Li would be gone. I never questioned her whereabouts, where she was until midnight, pretending to know nothing. I suspected things. She always kept secretive her movements and feelings when it came to boys. I was meant to know nothing.

One night I fell asleep hungry. Night comes by stealth no different than day surprises by creeping up on us. The colours about us fade to dark and the whispering songs of the soft breeze can be finally heard. Darkness made me sleepy. I was dreaming of fried catfish and steamed rice prepared by Li when I was awakened by someone at the door again. This time I stepped forward and opened it. It was Father. I could not believe it. I nearly collapsed on the flagstones. Without speaking he entered, took off his cap, the same one he had when he went away, and went to the stove for broth. Without a word he sat and commenced eating. I was too scared to speak, to ask where he had been? We all thought he had been killed in the war with the Japanese but weren't officially informed. Now he had just returned. He will know what to do...about Li, Johnny and the *Laowai*. Father will know. I only have to ask him, I thought. Father ate the broth slowly and mechanically as I watched. I would get Li, but I figured Li was a woman and the questions I wanted to ask Father were men's questions. I took some bread from the shelf and placed it beside his plate, but he didn't touch it. He ignored it completely.

He never even looked at me or said how big I had grown since he left. Did he not know who I was? Then I told him who I was, but he did not respond at all. Emboldened by this telling, I said more. Poured it all out. About Li, about Johnny, old Zhang, Tang, then about Père Olivier and his faith:

'What can I do about Li and Johnny?'

'What about Tang?'

'Should I or shouldn't I visit the *Laowai* priest?'

'I miss having no mother!'

'What am I to do, Pop? I am the man of the house now.'

He finished eating, put his cap on, and walked to the door, not speaking a word to me. I watched him walk away and wanted to run after him, but something wouldn't let me. Like I was being dragged back. I shouted for him to return. All of a sudden something heavy was on my chest and my eyes opened. The house and everything dissolved and there I was in my cot in the darkness. A big, fat, black cat was lying on my chest, there, in the dark. It must have come in my open window during the night. Never before had this happened. It lay upon me, watching my face and purring to itself. I had been dreaming again. But it was so real.

Some nights later when I again awoke in the chair to go to bed properly I noticed the door again unlatched. I peeped into Li's room. She wasn't there. This was happening all the time now, I knew. The unlatched door was a giveaway. What does all this mean? I thought. Where would she go at night? I decided then to wait in the chair for her to return.

Again, around midnight, the door crept open. I decided to pretend I was sleeping. I shut my eyes, but like a dog sleeps, I kept one eye half open, squinting to see. Li sneaked in, wearing a headscarf to hide her head. She saw me sleeping and went to the table to remove the scarf, then went to her room. But she left something on the table with her scarf. I could make out it looked heavy. While she was busy in her room, I opened my eyes and leapt up to see for myself what it was. It was a book of some kind. I looked at the cover, the writing in Chinese. It read *'HOLY CATECHISM OF THE CATHOLIC CHURCH'*. I recognised it immediately. It belonged to Père Olivier. It was the same book he was teaching to me.

One evening a heavy rainfall came. Summer rain. It lashed the roof and sidewalks of our street. I went round the back to check on Misha. I had tied her to a rock at night and fed her potato skins. She was now my dog. Misha appeared to be afraid this time. I thought it was the rain that made her uneasy or that rats may have frightened her and looked around, beating my feet on the ground to make enough noise to scare them away. Misha licked my hand. 'Good dog,' I said and I placed her in the shelter of the woodshed. She was still nervous as I left her.

When I went to go in again I smelled something coming from inside...smoke. But I had not yet lit the fire. Demons, I thought, fearful of Père Olivier's teachings, and the talk of the elders in our village of spirits. But it smelled more like cigarette tobacco.

I ran as fast as I could. I knew where I would go, where I would find them. Through the deserted village streets past homes with smoke wisps rising from chimney pipes. It was after supper time – late...and very wet.

I rounded the hut to approach from the back. The door was shut. I banged and banged in the rain. Père Olivier appeared behind the door when it opened. He had his small reading glasses perched on his nose and wore a button-up sweater that was open.

'Yes, boy?' he asked. He seemed calm. 'What is it?'

'I need to see Li,' I said. 'Now.'

Père Olivier glanced to his side and cleared his throat.

'Li is not here, boy.'

'Yes, she is. I know.'

'Can I help you?' he asked calmly.

'Li!' I shouted past him. 'Li, come quick. There is somebody in our house.'

I went to back away. In truth I was so frightened on my own.

Père Olivier stood aside and Li then appeared from behind him. She was holding a book.

'What's the matter?' she said, a concerned frown on her.

'Li, I think someone's at home.'

'What?'

'Yes, I heard noise. Then I smelled smoke – cigarettes!'

Li's face – first her eyes widened, then her face paled.

'Smoke? Are you certain? Who did you see?'

Then she lowered her voice and carefully looked around to see if anyone else was listening.

'I must go,' she said to Père Olivier.

'Wait, I'll go, too,' he said.

I followed as Li marched ahead with Père Olivier by her side. Thunder rattled the quiet sky and the rain burst down. Another downpour.

On the porch Li halted and sniffed the air. Even in the rain I smelled cigarettes. Did she? Père Olivier stepped forward and opened the latch. We were drenched. Inside, only the light from the fire illuminated the dark inside, flickering shapes on the walls. We entered. Silence and dark. Then, over in the easy chair, red dots of light like a fire moth circling...a cigarette tip. There was someone smoking a cigarette on the chair.

'Hello, Tang,' said Li. 'I thought I smelled a tiger. Your brand of smoke has given you away.'

I sat on the wet floorboards holding my cup of broth. Its onion aroma always made me hungry. Li was boiling water to make tea. Tang stood tall and straight backed. His gait immediately revealed him as a soldier. Yes, a soldier of Mao's Peoples' Liberation Army – the Reds. Père Olivier stood facing him, droplets of rainwater running from his hat's brim and his hair down his freckled face. Tang took out his packet of cigarettes, flicked one out and lit up. He offered Père Olivier one:

'No. Thank you,' the priest said.

Tang reached into the pot and ladled two bowls of broth. He offered one to Père Olivier. Père Olivier nodded respectfully and gratefully accepted a bowl. Both hands cradling it, he gulped a first slug of broth then appeared to relax.

Tang then opened his greatcoat and pulled a knife from his belt. He seized a loaf from a shelf and sliced it in half. Again he offered one half to Père Olivier. The priest took it and gently began to nibble at it, all the while looking into Tang's face as if searching for something.

'We believe in sharing, in distribution. That no-one should go hungry,' said Tang, calmly cutting pieces from his bread and chewing.

'Noble ideals,' said Père Olivier, nodding.

'We are closer than you think,' replied Tang. Then, as if being called back to the present, he added: 'Our armies, I mean. Won't be long now...Nanking, then Shanghai.'

Père Olivier seemed to calculate this.

'What does your scripture tell us?' Tang blurted out again. 'That man does not live by bread alone? Yet you clearly like bread, priest.'

Tang then sliced a heel of the loaf he was holding and chewed it, all the while scrutinizing the priest carefully.

'I agree,' he said. 'It is good bread.'

Père Olivier said nothing.

Tang rested his long fingers on the heavy, well-read book Père Olivier left on the table. He opened it and thumbed through the dog-eared thin pages. His eyes narrowed as he read along the small printed words using fingers to trace the lines. His face seemed captivated or excited, his brow looking cross.

'Ha ha,' he snorted then. 'Tell me, priest, can you explain this one...

"Cursed is the ground because of you;
Through painful toil you will eat food from it all the days of your
life.
It will produce thorns and thistles for you
and you will eat the plants of the field.
By the sweat of your brow you will eat your food
until you return to the ground
since from it you were taken
for dust you are
and into dust you will return"

'This is taken from Genesis,' Tang went on. 'So we are meant to work for our food till we sweat? We are sentenced to toil the earth, to labour here, until we eventually turn to dust? We suffer here, then we die? Let me tell you priest, socialist society will guarantee food and shelter for all, a life here on earth, not just an existence – a life *before* we die.'

'That's the punishment of our ancestors. We are all banished from Eden...the banished children of Eve,' said Père Olivier.

'For eating forbidden fruit?'

'For disobeying God.'

'You have an answer for all,' he said. 'Like all you men in black. You see, Father...I'm supposed to call you that, am I not? Father – even though you're not my father – or anybody else's I'm aware of,' he smiled. 'Of course you may be...you are a man,' he examined Père Olivier's face for a response. Then, 'I've come across you people before.'

He regarded Père Olivier suspiciously. 'Many times.' Then smiling, he said 'Jesuit. Am I right?'

Père Olivier gulped his broth slowly, his Adam's apple in and out as he swallowed, his blue eyes acknowledged the question. I thought to myself quietly in the corner, 'Jesuit?' Again a new word, another for my collection. Just like with the other ones, it intrigued me, its sound.

'You fellahs are the famous...or infamous Men in Black, the pope's army, the so-called stormtroopers of the Vatican. Or is it...' He turned to face Père Olivier. 'Of the Black Pope?'

Père Olivier did not answer. I was fascinated as I sat watching and learning. The open fire crackled in its hollow as Tang lifted more faggots and tossed them on for more heat. He rubbed his fingers along one stick and, grasping it, held it in the flame. It took fire. He lifted it out again and brought it to eye level. His narrow eyes examined it the way me and Zhu would study insects, grasshoppers, bugs. The stick burned for a bit then extinguished. Its smoke vanishing into the air.

'Ha,' said Tang. 'In the fire it burns with the rest, gives out heat. On its own it is useless...just like society without socialism, without fraternity. Together we work better than as individuals. Selfishness – the ruination of our nation.'

'Quite,' Père Olivier spoke at last. 'When we pray in communion with others, our prayer has greater power, greater effect for God's mercy and grace than on our own – "when two or more pray in my name" as holy scripture tells us.

Tang smiled, lifted his bowl up to salute the priest, sipped some broth, then said:

'Little sticks have their uses so. Someday I prophesise those who appear great before us will break their backs chopping sticks for us.'

'Uses? Yes, they make fire, they burn.'

Then Père Olivier said, 'You prophesise? Are you now a prophet as well? Even the great Lao Tzu never claimed to be a prophet, or maybe it is not prophesy but a policy you are describing.'

'Karl Marx.' answered Tang sharply.

'Marx is the prophet. Everything, everything you witness going on in the world today has been predicted by Karl Marx. In a brilliant work of over six hundred pages Marx has reasoned the causes behind human suffering scientifically – a diagnosis.'

'And,' he went on, 'given a prognosis. The current turmoil caused by global capitalism has been predicted by Marx, the prognosis: the dictatorship of the proletariat and peasants.'

'The fall of man in Eden is the cause of all human suffering,' said Père Olivier. 'Original sin.'

Tang's face blushed with what appeared rage.

'Are we to wallow in our suffering because of a mythology?'

'A metaphor,' said Père Olivier.

'Because of a story?'

'Human nature is inescapable.'

'So far,' said Tang. 'But some obvious solutions haven't yet been implemented. After the revolution there will be peace and justice. Then socialism. After a generation or so of socialism, the new socialist man will have overcome the temptations and corruption feudalism and capitalism has forced onto him, on his ancestors'

Tang laughed then and said, 'Doesn't your religion pray for the kingdom of god on Earth?'

'You promise us paradise now?' said Père Olivier. 'Paradise on Earth?'

'No,' said Tang, his face directed upwards. 'Earth on Earth. A world for men.'

'Everything in this world?' Père Olivier said. 'When I look around me I see war, murder, chaos, madness.'

'That's what happens when you are expelled from Eden.' Tang smiled.

'Apocalypse? Does your good book not predict such things? Why be afraid if you will be saved?'

Père Olivier turns his face to the fire, his cheek reddened with its heat.

'I'm not,' he spoke. Then he said nothing more.

'I know,' he added.

I felt scared. I shivered and it wasn't cold.

'Religion,' said Tang then, 'is the opium of the people – Karl Marx wrote that.'

'No,' said Père Olivier. 'Opium is the opium of the people. As a Chinese you should know.'

'Isn't there a Christian hymn that goes "all things bright and beautiful, all creatures great and small, the lord god made them all"?'

'Yes,' said Père Olivier.

'And it goes on "the rich man in his castle, the poor man in his...something something".'

'A protestant hymn.' said Père Olivier.

'Well we know now that creatures evolved, and were not "created", and so did the rich man only achieve wealth at the expense and most likely the deaths of many poor men – unless you believe God willed all this?'

'It is a protestant hymn,' said Père Olivier, 'and its sentiments are anachronistic now.'

'Anachronistic? More like archaic,' said Tang with disgust.

'Like your God...archaic. God is history as Marx said. History's dialectic moves things along a direction...a path, not a God.'

'I mean if Christian songs extol injustice like the one I just quoted.'

'Christians do not extol injustice, not my Order anyway.'

'Oh? Right and wrong is it for you, then? Right and wrong! Rules and commandments!'

'No,' said Père Olivier. 'Not right and wrong, that's too simple.'

'What then?' demanded Tang.

'Good and evil,' said Père Olivier.

Tang could not answer this. I could see his expression look blank. He reached for the bible and flung it at the wall then he lit up another *Tiger*. He paced the room not speaking. I was feeling drowsy, my eyelids heavy, but did not want sleep just yet. So I shut my eyes, listening. There was a tense silence.

Père Olivier ate some more broth from his bowl then placed it on the table, bowed respectively, placed his hat on his head, and left the house.

'He knows too much about nothing,' Tang said, sounding uneasy.

Li came with tea. 'Knowledge is power,' she said. 'You taught me.'

Tang gave her a trusting look. 'I taught you to read. Remember?'

'You taught me more than to read, Tang.'

'I taught you more than reading?'

Her voice quivered a little. 'Yes, Tang...*you* know.'

'I know the ways of the world. I taught you these?'

'You taught me more than these, Tang.'

'This world is ugly. Cruel. Brutal. Everything a struggle. This I realised from early on. I think I told you only Marx has the answer. And through Mao we get to Marx...'

'Yes, you told me. You truly believe this?'

'I believe.'

Tang then chewed his lower lip.

'You taught me more than that, Tang' she said softly. Her voice sounded different to me then – more gentle. Curious, I squeezed an eye open. She approached him slowly and he squeezed her close.

When I awoke the next day, he was gone and Li was asleep on the floor.

Johnny wrote Zhang a second letter and it came like the first by a despatch rider on a horse. It was morning before we went out on The River.

Before we ever set out, the sampan with old Zhou passed our village's moorings.

'Ahoy, does Lao have anything to say about early mornings that you object to, Zhang-ze?' he shouted over to us.

'I am Lao, why not ask me?' Lao said angrily.

'Yes, Lao, you are some philosopher...like your illustrious namesake.'

Zhang spat, 'If he did you wouldn't know anyway.'

'Ah, but I know when to rise,' Zhou shouted back. 'I don't sleep with an empty jug beside me. I have my woman to mind me.'

'She mustn't be any good, then, if you leave your bed early each morning.'

Zhou gave a wave back in teasing fashion pretending not to hear, and his crew laughed.

Old Mister Xi was busy sorting out the letters – only two came this time; Johnny's was one.

Before we went out, Zhang asked to visit Père Olivier ("that *Laowai* priest merchant") to listen to the letter being read to him. I knew Père Olivier would be saying his mass and doing his usual motions, so I said it was better to wait.

'Wait? And leave the fish to Zhou?'

'Fish breed,' said Lao. 'There will be plenty'

'That Zhou,' said Zhang with grinding teeth. 'He is greedy. To come up to our village waters…'

'*I* will bring the *Laowai*,' I said then.

So I walked off to fetch Père Olivier.

Dear Uncle,

I hope you are well and fishing is good. There should be plenty fish now in The River.

Please tell me how is Li? Is she well? But please do not mention I asked.

Me, I am still here. This war is very frightening. Unending noise of gunshot by day and pounding artillery by night.

We came to a village not unlike Zhaoui last week. It had been destroyed by the Communists, we were told. Those enemies of our great nation!

Dead bodies lay everywhere along with dead dogs, in pools of blood. Smoke rose from the ashes of huts. Captain Hu took me and Wu zhi, another soldier, aside and told us he had a special duty for us. We were marched around to the rear of some shacks still standing. There, another soldier stood guard over two captured Red Army prisoners. 'Dogs,' I first thought.

The Captain signalled to the guard to leave us alone. Then he read a statement to the two prisoners – young boys of maybe eighteen – saying they were to be executed as spies.

The boys listened to every word in stoic silence. Captain Hu then finished his pronouncement, ordered myself and Wu zhi to shoot the prisoners. To execute them in the name of the Republic of China.

Wu zhi and I looked at each other, reading each other's' eyes.

I will be honest, Dear Uncle, I may have killed men in this war from a great distance, at least I think I have. But here I was only one metre from a man – a boy I was ordered to kill.

Captain Hu made the prisoners kneel with their backs presented to us. He made them bow their heads. Captain Hu ordered us to take aim. I lifted my heavy rifle up, Wu zhi followed. Then I saw one of the prisoners, just a lad really, begin to tremble with fear. He pissed himself.

Captain Hu ordered 'FIRE'. Wu zhi looked at me then fired his gun and the prisoner in front dropped dead, blood hosing from his skull. Smoke and cordite from the gun stank. But I could not fire.

My Red Army prisoner was in spasms by this stage, terrified. I could actually smell shit. Then we heard a loud crack. Captain Hu had fired his revolver into the prisoner, finishing the job I was ordered to do. I felt such shame. And the stench.

It was truly awful, Dear Uncle. It is truly a terrible thing, this war.

I was truly horrified by this letter. This is war? This is not the war I played with Zhu. Père Olivier made the sign of the cross and removed his glasses, clearly ill at ease.

Zhang looked vacant and wet-eyed, and said nothing at first.

'Thank you,' he said to Père Olivier, and bowed. Père Olivier then handed him the letter. Zhang took it slowly, looking at it without understanding its symbols. He folded it up and put it in his pocket. Then we did not fish that day. Instead I went home but did not tell Li. Not this time.

Another evening, after my leaving of Père Olivier, on my walk home I began thinking about God and other things. You see, Père Olivier called God 'Lord' or 'The Lord', yet our new Republic had forbidden titles like 'Emperor' and 'Lord', so Li told me. We have no lords now except those we elect or appoint. Except Mayor Xi who wasn't elected but was not a lord also. This began to puzzle me. In our Republic, we choose our leaders, so we are told. It is democracy, a word I have to practice. We do not deliberately choose God – he is there according to Père Olivier – our Lord!

Then it occurred to me, we must also elect our Gods – God or Buddha, Jesus, Allah. We choose these to be our God, or have they chosen us? Or are these fake or real? Is the heaven Père Olivier talks about a democracy or a kingdom? These were the questions running through my head that evening.

To avoid Zhou this one day, old Zhang-ze ordered us up early to take the boat upriver where fish were meant to be plentiful and we could catch the shoals before they swam down The River. We punted and sailed up it fighting the downstream current all the way. The River can be wide as a sea, so we were taught since childhood, but it narrows as well, I learned. The River bent at points with long grassy banks and overhanging branches at the narrow points. There was the echo of monkey noises from within the jungled banks, of parrots and other animals I did not know. I felt very excited – an adventurer. Zhu will be envious, I thought.

'This is all new to me,' Lao said. 'I've never fished this far from the village.'

We took in much fish that morning. So much so that old Zhang said we would go farther upriver. We sailed around a bend. It was not as hot on this stretch of river, there was no baking sun to roast us because of the shades of the vegetation. It was, however, tropical, and felt humid. We sailed on upriver. Around midday, the heat got so intense we could hardly work. The jungle noises also became fewer. Lao noticed it first:

'They've all gone for a midday rest,' he said. 'Animals are smart. Smarter than us sometimes.'

Zhang said nothing, just grunted and spat into the water.

We floated along on dead water till it became exhausting to strain ourselves fishing in the heat. Our catch had been good though for that early in the day – there was good fishing upriver.

'This is uncharted water,' said Lao, 'Can we take a rest from the sun?' he asked Zhang.

Zhang reached for a cigarette, lit one up, and considered. His eyes narrowed against the glare of midday as he surveyed the banks alongside us. Then he asked:

'Do you want to see gold?'

Me and Lao looked at each other then nodded to Zhang.

'Come on,' he said. 'Over here.'

We shipped against the spot chosen by Zhang. When we had tied the skiff to an overhanging tree, Zhang said to follow him. The foliage was thick here and overgrown. Zhang led us, brushing behind him the spindling branches and vine creepers. I was lucky I wasn't tall because once or twice the recoiling branches struck Lao, who cursed each time it happened. Once, though, as I passed a gap in the trees, a huge bough came from nowhere and smacked me in the head. I fell down and felt the shock, shame, the pain, ringing ears. Lao helped me up laughing. 'I'm so sorry,' he said. 'I couldn't resist it.'

He had actually bent the bough back like a giant catapult, and when the tension was so much he let go to deliberately strike me.

'Just be careful on the way back,' he said, still laughing.

Old Zhang was way ahead of us now.

We had not to wander very far when Zhang stopped in his tracks and looked upward. We had reached a clearance and the blue sky was visible once again. But it wasn't the sky that made us look up. There it was, yes, overgrown with vegetation, but still wonderful. I had not seen one before, or since: a real Pagoda.

I had learned and heard tell of these, and even of some constructed in gold. This appeared wooden but beautifully crafted. There was something about it...we all approached closer. Yes, I thought, there was gold gilt on parts of it.

'Is it real?' Lao asked, climbing up to test.

'It must be,' Zhang answered. 'It is there for centuries and nobody has stolen it. The ground here is meant to be sacred. This is a famous one, this Pagoda.'

'I have not heard of this,' said Lao.

'I have only been here once before,' said Zhang. 'When I was a boy – a little older than you,' he said to me.

I looked around me at this tiered structure with gilt ornament embedded. True, there were vines and brambles outgrowing from within and around it.

'It hasn't been occupied for centuries,' said Zhang.

'Who built it?' I asked.

'Monks,' he said. 'You can tell your *Laowai* priest this was around a thousand years before his religion,' he said with sarcasm, spitting then.

I climbed up the steps and went to explore.

'Careful,' he shouted after me. 'There will be snakes lying asleep. Don't disturb any or you'll regret it!'

I quickly jumped back down again. Lao was busy tapping the gold gilt edges out of curiosity.

'Gold? Why has no one stolen it all?'

'Bad luck, superstition, honour among thieves...many reasons,' said Zhang.

'Can we go inside?' Lao asked.

'You can,' said Zhang. 'But I wouldn't.'

'Snakes?' I said, worried.

'Snakes, rats, and who knows what else resides in there,' Zhang said, squinting up at the tower. 'A serpent's lair...decorated in gold!'

We stood in its shade. The high midday sun was just beyond the Pagoda now moving westwards, causing a shadow over us. We sat in the cool shade chatting in general. Zhang and Lao smoked.

A while or so passed. The sun still shone and by now the familiar jungle noises restarted; it was well past midday now. After an hour or so passed, Zhang got restless:

'Let's be getting back, we've had our rest,' he said.

Lao moaned out loud.

'*"The truth is not always beautiful, nor beautiful words the truth"*, Lao Tzu says,' Zhang said again.

'A wise man indeed.'

This voice wasn't Lao or Zhang. We looked up. We were surrounded by them. Eight in all. All armed with blades – swords, knives, and the like – circling us. The one in command, the leader, who spoke, was holding a pistol.

Zhang swore some curse with a jerk of his head, as if blaming himself. The leader heard this.

'Not nice,' he said. 'What would Lao say?' His accent was rural. The others did not speak, they were either grinning or serious-looking, concentrating on us. They were all small in stature except for one giant of a man. They all had bald shaven skulls. They wore no sandals or shirts, only trouser pants. I never saw their like before or since.

'Bandits,' Lao whispered to me. We stood up at once as if by instinct. The bandit leader held his pistol to Zhang.

'Which tribe are you?' he asked him.

Zhang said nothing.

'Where are you coming from?' he asked. Again Zhang did not answer. The bandit cocked his pistol at Zhang's head.

'Huhji,' said Zhang gesturing southwards with his head. Clever, I thought.

'Then you are far away,' said the bandit. 'You will not get home tonight.'

He approached us closer.

'Many tribes and warlords pay a hefty price for strong labour.' He looked us over with careful scrutiny. He went to Lao first, felt his arm from wrist up to shoulder.

'Strong,' he said. 'And young.' Backing away, he said, 'They will pay much for you.'

Then he looked at Zhang, who stared straight ahead, keeping silent. I myself thought Zhang would have some answer to give the bandit, some Lao Tzu, but no, he kept tight-lipped throughout. The bandit leered at him, also saying nothing, then:

'An old buck – can't be taught new tricks.'

The bandit then went to feel Zhang's arm, but old Zhang recoiled. The bandit stood back as if expecting a blow, then he smiled:

'Strong still...I can see it in him. Spirited, too. Might have to dispose of this one yet.'

Then he stood in front of me, taking me in with lively, darting, bloodshot eyes.

'Only a kid...be different if he were a girl. Still, might fetch a good price in Shanghai, there are a lot of those types there.'

Zhang spat on the ground, an enormous greener from the back of his throat. The bandit turned to him.

'Have you food?'

Zhang just shook his head.

'I thought so,' said the bandit, looking around us for signs. 'Neither have we. We were actually hunting when we found you.' He gestured with his head to somewhere beyond the trees. 'Our boat is not far away.'

Pirates, I thought then. It made sense.

'Well, we cannot eat you tonight, even though you are now our guests.' He grinned at the others when he said this, but they did not react at first; only when he smiled did they also laugh. Some had rotten teeth. These men were truly scary to me. My heart was beating and I wanted to cry. I wanted to go home to Li.

'We can't risk you to come hunting with us – there's this wild pig we're on the trail of and we don't want to lose it. But you are our guests – you will earn us much.'

Neither of us spoke. I wanted Li.

Then he roared at his men in a foreign dialect I did not understand. The giant of a man, who must have been as tall as a tree, came forward. He wore a wide leather belt around his waist with two knives inside. His body was shining with perspiration. What now? I wondered. The leader gave him another pistol from his holster and again spoke in this foreign or strange dialect. The big pirate grunted and nodded, then fixed the gun on us.

The pirate leader grinned at Zhang:

'Riko here will keep you company till we return with our catch. Later you will join us for supper and watch us eat pig.' He stuttered his words as if our tongue was strange to him.

'Sit,' he ordered us. 'Sit on the grass.'

Slowly we obeyed him.

'Raise your arms.'

We obeyed this, too. Then some more words to Riko before disappearing into the bush with the rest of his gang.

We sat quietly for a bit at first, relieved they were gone. Riko, however, towered tall over us pointing the gun. Zhang whispered to Lao about these men being pirates foraging ashore. Riko shouted at him in his foreign dialect. Zhang and Lao looked at each other. Zhang grunted under his breath that Riko 'this goon' was the term he used, 'doesn't understand our lingo'. Lao nodded understanding without looking directly at Zhang.

After a few minutes, Lao put his arm down and Riko shouted something unintelligible at him, waving his gun. Lao indicated he wanted a cigarette, making smoking sign language. Riko stared at him intensely but gave a nod. Lao took out his packet of cigarettes. There was one left. He put it in his mouth and threw away the pack. Riko glanced at it. *Lucky Strike*, American cigarettes...where did Lao get them, I wondered?

Riko bent down to examine the pack while still pointing the gun. He shook the pack; nothing. It was empty, sure enough. Old Zhang then whispered to Lao:

'Look at his fingers...yellow from smokes. This guy needs a smoke badly, I'll bet on it.'

Riko blasted away some more words at Zhang to shut up. Lao smoked his cigarette hungrily. Riko glared and frowned at him, then to the empty packet lying on the ground.

'I've got an idea,' said Zhang, who was studying all this.

'I hope so,' whispered Lao. 'Won't be long till the others come back, I reckon.'

Zhang signalled to Riko that he wanted to smoke, too. Riko aimed the gun at him. Zhang, using sign language, asked Riko if *he* would like a cigarette. Riko looked puzzled, still pointing the gun. Still making gestures, Zhang showed Riko he too had no cigarettes left. Riko croaked some more unintelligible words at us.

But Lao kept on smoking, making it seem so pleasurable. I could only watch as Riko licked his dry lips and turned his head away. Zhang whispered, 'He's gasping for a smoke. Keep it up.'

Then Lao took an enormous drag on his cigarette and flung the used stub away from him. Riko spotted this, and rushed over to take it up and desperately smoke the last bit of it. Zhang winked at us.

When Riko finished, Zhang indicated there were no more cigarettes. Riko again looked puzzled. Zhang pointed at the discarded packet of Lucky Strikes. Riko took notice. Using understandable sign language and gestures, Zhang indicated there were more cigarettes, but not with us right now. Why, even I could read what Zhang was communicating to Riko. Riko aimed his gun at Zhang as if to say, 'shut up'.

Zhang raised his arms to say, 'Okay, I give up'.

A minute or so later, Riko grunted something. He pointed to the empty pack. Zhang quickly nodded.

'There's more where that came from.' 'Over there,' he indicated towards the bush in the direction we had come from the river. Then he asked Riko, 'You want more?' indicating a raft of cigarettes to be had.

Riko reached out and grabbed Zhang by the neck. I thought he would kill him, that Zhang had gone too far. But instead, he pointed Zhang towards the bushes and followed with the gun trained on him. Then, as if he forgot something, he looked back at me and Lao. Waving his pistol, he ordered us to move along, too, in front of him.

We kept our arms up while walking along. In the thickets this was difficult but each time we lowered our hands Riko shouted at us and clicked his gun. The suspense whenever he did this was truly frightening; it could go off anytime. On we stumbled till Riko stopped us and seemed to demand where these cigarettes were. Zhang pointed straight ahead. Suspicious now, Riko marched us forwards, himself taking up the rear. Then Zhang called to Lao:

'Ready, Lao.'

I did not notice it but we had reached the spot where Lao had bent back that springy bough and hit me with it. Zhang took me ahead with him. Lao followed us, then Riko.

Suddenly, I heard it; a huge impact sound. Riko groaned and let off a piercing shot from the pistol.

'Run,' said Lao.

We all three ran on ahead over tree roots and dense foliage. The path was now recognisable as the one we had come. Finally we saw our skiff, and when we reached it, Lao untied it. We pushed off from the bank and out onto The River again.

Lao was bursting with laughter and excitement:

'I got him good.'

'Yeah,' said Zhang, 'I heard it.'

'Right in the balls,' said Lao.

'Ouch,' said Zhang, gripping his crotch. 'Big man Riko.'

Once on board we went back to sailing normally again. We reached a wide section of water once again.

After some time, a lone sail appeared up front. Old Zhang squinted his eyes towards it, gripping his stubbly chin as if calculating. He spat overboard. 'Just a Junk,' he grunted as if disappointed.

Lao looked at me with concern.

'This is unchartered water for us, we ought to head towards home,' he muttered to me.

The oncoming Junk became bigger. I thought I could hear pounding, drumbeats. Then Zhang quickly about-turned:

'Dammit!' he said. 'Backwards, go back.'

'What is it?' Lao asked.

'It's pirates,' said Zhang. 'And they're onto us.'

Lao swore, then rushed to alter course to sail back downriver. Zhang spat, gripping rope with his fist.

'I should have known they'd come,' he grunted to himself. I went to help but tripped over nets – I had learned to fish, not to handle a boat. I felt my ankle swell and ache.

'If they see we're only fishermen, perhaps they'll leave us alone. But they know we've spotted them, that they're there. They might not wish to be known. It might be our friends we just left who don't want us to leave,' Zhang added.

River pirates preyed on trading vessels as well being the scourge of small villages along their way.

All I could do was watch. My foot hurt. The sails of this oncoming Junk shimmered closer and closer on the river's horizon in the haze of the hot sun, which reappeared above us on this wide stretch of the River once again. It seemed like a floating mirage – perhaps it was? Only those drumbeats thumping even louder now and rising in tempo like my heartbeat confirmed it was real. I imagined I heard them, the pirates, swearing, yelling all sorts of tortures and obscenities. The voices sounded terrifying. Then I saw them. A sight that still gives me shivers when I think of it. They were naked, their bodies glistened in the sun's heat, wearing bands tied around their heads and belts with weapons attached. They moved like ants about the junk, their voices shouting   orders and threats. This only added to the fierceness of their bodies' movements. I squinted my eyes against the sun's light reflected on the water. To see them better. There is something about fear that freezes one in the moment, that attracts one to fear, that brings fear on. I could see that they were almost all bald-shaven – the way me and Zhu always imagined them.

They scurried around their vessel gesticulating like madmen, beating drums. I thought they might very well be demons.

Our plain fishing skiff had but the single advantage that it was maybe two hundred metres in front of the pirate Junk when we made our getaway. Plain sailing they could catch us easily. However, another advantage opened up once we re-entered the narrow bendy points once again. Here, the river narrowed and twisted. There was also dense foliage on each bank to negotiate. Here the Junk would have difficulties catching up.

Lao punted using both oars, while Zhang managed the tiller, navigating us. My job was to pull the sails' according to Zhang's instructions.

Zhang was hauling the net. It was heavy with water and fish weighing it down causing it to drag. But old uncle Zhang was strong. The river carried us along. We were going in the direction of the stream to return to the village. Lao was punting away with his rods while I assisted Zhang.

'It's our weight,' said Zhang. 'We must dump our catch.'

Lao looked around astonished. 'But our day's work? Our food?'

'You want to be lunch for those guys,' Zhang said to him, pointing in the direction of the Junk.

As we entered the narrow stretch of river the drumbeats from the Junk in pursuit faded a bit. I hoped they had quit. Soon the Junk would be in the same stretch of water. This will slow them down, we thought.

First, we had to outrace the pirate Junk on the wide open river to steer it back to the narrow bendy stretch of river with all its jungle and vegetation. Zhang cut the nets adrift, setting us free from the drag of our full day's plentiful fishing. Lao looked at me helpless, and, I could tell he was angry. We watched as our big net, brim full of fish, silver, grey, red, was set adrift and disappeared below, dissolving into the river's surface – feeding for the crabs and other shellfish – the river's underwater scavengers. Once while playing, myself and Zhu witnessed the spectacle of crabs attacking a dead fish. They made such an orgy of feasting on it, it was reduced to bone in minutes. One giant crab we saw even jealously defended a portion of the carcass for himself, fighting other crabs away. I often wondered at the intelligence of these creatures. And nature at work.

'I'm not losing this,' said Lao, indicating the fish our rods had caught. He quickly cast them up onboard and covered them.

'Hoist the sail,' roared old Zhang. 'Let us get speed.'

I pulled the rope to raise the mainsail. There was little wind in the day's heat but our craft was small and our sail wide so it assisted somewhat in keeping us in front. The drumbeats sounded terrifying as the Junk closed the distance. Lao kept looking behind and rowed faster every time. I gripped the mainsail ropes as tight as I could, leaning overboard, and Zhang shouted his orders. The current carried us at a rapid pace round the first bend.

'We will outrun them,' Zhang said with confidence in his grey-stubble jowls.

'The current works for them, too,' shouted Lao, not yet convinced.

The monkey chatter had ceased where once we could hear it, same for other wildlife. A bad omen, I believed.

'If we keep close to the bank we can progress faster,' said Zhu. 'That way we won't be caught in middle drift and we save effort.'

'Alright,' said Lao. 'You're the skipper.' I overheard him say to himself, 'My arse...big mistake going this far upriver!'

Lao then rowed starboard along the river bank, while Zhang steered the course. By now we couldn't see the tailing Junk, it was somewhere out of sight. We could, however, still hear the pounding drums. Enough to know it was still in pursuit.

'They must want us pretty bad,' Lao said.

'We are the evidence they are there. They want to destroy all trace. We know too much,' said Zhang.

I felt horror at this. My blood ran cold. What could I do? It was then I recalled Père Olivier's teachings and what it was he professed. So, then I offered a silent prayer begging God to deliver us.

'What are you doing, boy?' Zhang was shouting. 'Lower the mast – the branches.'

I had neglected to notice the branches and riverside growth. There were overhanging trees at another bend in the river. Our single mast wasn't lowered as it should have been, for there was little or no wind or need for the sail or space for the mast in the overgrown thickets bankside.

I leapt up to lower the main mast rope but then a huge overhanging tree bough collided with our yard arm. The mainsail tumbled. Collapsed. I doubled out of its way. There was a roar to my rear. Someone in pain. I saw Lao look behind me then rush from his post. I turned to see. Zhang lay flat on the deck, blood spurting from his right arm...or where his arm should be.

'The boom has severed his arm,' shouted Lao. I stared as blood filled the deck bright red. Zhang appeared conscious but wasn't responding to anything. A blood red bone was sticking out from his arm's stump like fresh meat. No right hand. It lay on the red soaked deck, twitching all of itself.

The bough had cut our mast, and in the collision Zhang's arm was caught by the boom when it collapsed. When the mast was felled by the moving tree above on the riverbank, the arm was crushed and severed. I heard the drumbeats intensify. Things were getting much worse now.

Zhang lay there gasping. I surely thought he would die. His chest was swelling up and down with his other arm lying across it. The skiff came onto a wider stretch of the river now, and the Junk sounded like it was still in pursuit.

Lao pressed down on Zhang's wound to try to stop the blood pumping out. We were adrift by this stage, no one steering or guiding us. We saw the pirates come round the bend. They had us. Where was that prayer I said?

As the familiar drumbeats got louder and more intense the sounds changed. Firecrackers? Were they now firing on us?

I bowed my head to pray, for I was sure I was facing my death.

'Look,' said Lao, pointing.

The Junk's sails were shredded. Then we saw pirates either fall or leap into the river. What was this? More sounds.

'Look,' shouted Lao again. 'A patrol.' He pointed at the steep bank overlooking us. An army patrol was firing down on the pirate Junk. Lao raised his fist and cheered. I felt the tears in my eyes.

'They sailed too far downriver,' said Lao. 'That was *their* mistake.'

Within a matter of a few minutes the Junk was destroyed. It remained half on fire, or half-   submerged. When Lao took control of our craft and we moved on towards home, I glanced upwards to the hill. An army officer gave us a wave. But I wasn't sure which side they were, which army.

Blood quelled from the gaping wound, old Zhang still gasped heavily. He was half unconscious, I thought.

'I am alive?' he asked.

'Yes, Zhang,' I answered.

He crossed his left arm to feel his other half limb and kept it there.

'Truly I am cursed,' he groaned. This curse again, I thought.

'I will most definitely need a woman now.'

Whether these two statements were meant to be related I do not know.

'Listen to me,' Lao said to me later. 'The old man was losing it. By going upriver, by dumping our catch, but first, by not standing up to Zhou, that bastard.'

On arriving in the village, help was called for Zhang. Père Olivier was summoned. Everyone stood around talking about what happened. Lao did all the talking.

'Pirates so near our village?' Old Mister Xi exclaimed. 'We definitely need the military to guard us now.'

Père Olivier knew something of medicine. There were no doctors around. Li also helped nurse the wound.

'Johnny must know,' she said to Zhang. 'Someone must tell him. He will be needed here now.'

'But where is he?' someone asked.

'He is away fighting for the cause,' said Mister Xi. 'A hero of our village.'

They placed Zhang on a blanket to tend him properly. Then, there started another commotion: dogs yapping and people running to see what was up now. The dust rose on the main street as a group of what looked like stragglers, each propping each other up, had appeared on the street. There were three of them; the one in the centre being held up by the other two.

'Who are these?'

'Where did they come from?'

The village kids swarmed about them and the dogs were taking turns at running in, yapping, then running away again.

'Look,' said one man. 'They are soldiers.'

Sure enough, although ragged, they were wearing the uniform of the Kuomintang. Mister Xi stomped across to greet them.

'Welcome to our brave army.' He bowed in friendly gesture.

The middle one collapsed onto the ground and the one on the right went to help him stand again. The soldier on the left reached into his tunic breast pocket and produced a worn-looking piece of paper. All three were breathless and clearly exhausted.

'Help yourselves to our food and water,' said Xi. The mayor snapped his fingers.

'Some tea. Bring some tea,' he said.

The tall soldier on the left waved his piece of tattered paper and asked:

'Who is Zhang-ze?'

The people stood back from the circle that had formed around the three men, widening the space. Nobody answered. Mayor Xi coughed, then said, 'Who's asking?'

'This is Zhaoui village?' the soldier asked.

Mayor Xi nodded it was.

'I bear here a letter for Zhang-ze. It's from his nephew.'

Everybody gasped at this.

'From Johnny,' went about the crowd.

'He is dead,' a woman said.

The crowd parted and a path was cleared down to old Zhang, who still lay on a blanket where he was tended by Li and Père Olivier. Mayor Xi said:

'Thank you. I will bring the letter to Zhang-ze.'

'No, 'the soldier said. 'I'm meant to hand it over personally to him. I have given my word.'

'Ah, a top military despatch,' said Xi. 'That gentleman lying over there is Zhang-ze, the man you seek. As you can see he has been gravely wounded in service to our village of Zhaoui.' Mister Xi pointed to Zhang, who had his eyes closed muttering to himself just like Père Olivier did with his beads and black leather book.

The tall soldier seemed shocked. He looked around for someone to confirm this was the case, that this was really Uncle Zhang. Heads in the populace nodded as if reading his mind.

He then walked towards Zhang, bent down, and placed the tattered letter in Zhang's good hand.

'You are Zhang-ze?'

Old Zhang's moist eyes blinked. He nodded his hairy face. Li rested her hand on the soldier's forearm.' Johnny? He is...alive?'

The soldier whispered, 'Yes.' Li put her fist in her mouth and held back tears. The soldier then whispered to Zhang.

'This letter was given to me by your nephew, Johnny, who served in action with us. He instructed me to give you it.'

When he got back to his feet, the soldier dusted himself off and returned to his two comrades, who were now devouring fruit and drinking tea.

'Please mention our village and our brave sons in Nanking,' said Mister Xi, bowing again.

'Nanking?' said the soldier, looking at his comrades, who each shot knowing looks back.

'Yes, Nanking...our capital.'

'You...have not heard?' said the soldier.

'Heard what?'

Again the three soldiers looked at each other.

'Nanking has fallen – it's fallen to the Communists!'

There was then a loud gasp from the crowd.

'What?'

'Yes, what?'

'Nanking is no longer the capital, it's fallen to the Reds.'

'When was this?'

'Three days now.'

People looked at each other, shocked by this news.

'They will eat our children,' one woman sobbed.

'Bastards,' said someone else.

'What about our boys who have gone off to fight?' asked another.

'Yes...like Johnny.'

'Now, now,' said Mayor Xi, trying to calm everyone. 'Johnny lives – and I am certain so do the others.

'Go, gentlemen, and wash, refresh yourselves. You are most welcome to rest here,' he said to the three soldiers.

Zhang was then taken back to his home in a stretcher. Li, myself, and Père Olivier went, too. Lao was back again busy spinning the yarn about the pirates to everyone, and of course, his role in it.

Zhang's home was a mess. It was untidy to say the least. Rice that looked ancient stained the plates. Aromas of fish abounded of course. Nets hung from rafters, fish hooks hung on threads. Zhang did not appear to eat any vegetables. Empty jugs of rice wine lay scattered about.

Li made hot tea. Père Olivier tended to the wound.

'He will live,' he said, 'but he will not fish again.'

Old Zhang heard this. He spat blood on the floor, saying, '"*The journey of a thousand miles begins with a single step*"– Lao Tzu.'

'You are conscious,' said Père Olivier. 'I am glad.'

'Fuck! I would rather be dead!'

'No, you wouldn't,' said Père Olivier.

'And what's that woman doing in my house?' Zhang demanded to know of Li. He gripped his bandaged arm stump with a grimace of obvious pain.

'Women!'

Li gave him his tea and said nothing. Her silences could speak volumes, I knew.

'It's more than tea I need now. Bring me wine, American whiskey.'

Père Olivier spoke: 'Now you are settled, Zhang, I think we ought to read this...'

'No religion,' said Zhang. 'No prayers!'

'No,' said Père Olivier, 'it's the letter from your nephew. Someone who was in the army with him delivered it personally...a friend, possibly. This is not from the military despatch,' he said.

'A final letter, do you think?' Li asked, surprised. 'What has happened?'

'Read it to me,' said Zhang. 'If cursed I am let it all come out at once.' He gave the worn-looking paper to Père Olivier.

I sat in a corner on a stool, sipping tea Li had made.

Again, Père Olivier put on his glasses and opened the creased note:

Dear Uncle,

Forgive my sentiments in this letter. I will understand it if you no longer wish to hear from me or look upon me again. It is simple. I could not take the war anymore. I could not stand it. All the killing. I have seen many deaths, my comrades included. I myself have killed.

If, as you have said many times, if there is a family curse on us, then I am the proof. My hands are stained with blood. The blood of Communists alright, but I have witnessed scenes I can no longer take in.

I have decided to leave, to run away. The city is not far and I'm going to hide there.

I can no longer return to Zhaoui, obviously. You must understand my position, dear Uncle.

Please try to understand and forgive your nephew.

I watched as Zhang's face looked motionless and dumb. He held back invisible tears. He rolled his head to the side and he motioned us to leave him.

Outside, Li said:

'He needs help...someone.'

'Johnny?'

'Yes, Johnny.'

'Johnny isn't here. He's deserted, run away. He's in the city,' I said.

'Shanghai is the nearest Nationalist city. The Communists have taken Nanking, and are approaching Shanghai from the west,' Père Olivier said.

'Then we need to go to Shanghai,' said Li.

'Isn't he a deserter?' I asked.

'The fact that his uncle is seriously injured means Johnny has a legitimate excuse to return home. He can say he's urgently needed at home. And after all, Johnny was only a volunteer soldier, he wasn't an enlisted one,' Père Olivier said.

'This will work?' Li asked.

'We first need to travel to Shanghai to find Johnny.'

'Through the hills?' I said, and stared upwards towards those hills but the blinding sun was shielding them.

'I am ready to go tomorrow, then,' said Père Olivier.

'Me too,' said Li.

'I would advise not to,' Père Olivier said. 'What of the gossip if a woman left the village with me? And when we return with Johnny, what will be said then? Or expected?'

Li considered this counsel, her face frowning.

'Yes,' she said, 'but if Johnny is there, he will hardly return with you. I must go.'

Père Olivier shook his head, 'I know of these things. Best not to.'

'I will go,' I spoke up.

They looked at me.

'That's settled, then,' said Père Olivier. 'We leave at dawn.'

'Alright,' said Li. 'I will write a letter for you to give to Johnny. He will come then.'

That night I slept little but prayed that we would survive those hills. Those hills that dominated the view from our village, and dominated my thoughts forever, it seemed.

The first thing I noticed about the forest was how cool it was. That searing sun that overlooked our village like a gigantic shimmering ball, was nowhere to be seen or experienced within the dank trees. An evergreen hue seemed everywhere, and the place smelled alive and sweet. The hills rose up from the earth into one dominating mound overlooking us below. An earthen giant formed from the landscape lording over creation.

Speckled daylight, visible through gaps in the ceiling of leafy boughs of the tall trees, lit our way. As we walked on soft, grassy soil, Père Olivier led the way, his characteristic rucksack on his shoulders. He didn't appear to hesitate; it was as if he knew exactly where we were going, or was being guided. It was all silent. I was expecting animal sounds. Perhaps the spirits only came out at night.

After about half an hour walking, the ground became less grassy and more brown dirt, more lumpy, too. We had to step over fallen trunks and I caught my foot on tree roots sticking out from the earth a couple of times. Our path got steeper, too – we were climbing higher. Whenever I looked behind to see down, all I saw were tree trunks. I couldn't look out upon our village the way I often imagined the Communists did to watch us.

On we trekked. Although the hills are not exceptionally steep, their slope being gradually upwards, I was still out of breath on my climb. Stepping on loose stones, over tree trunks and fallen boughs strewn in our path and feet lodging in dense earth took a lot of energy. For a route never before taken has no track and I was certain nobody had walked this way before. No human anyway. But Père Olivier seemed determined, so we followed, me and Misha, wherever he was leading us.

Before night, Père Olivier had me gather sticks to start a fire. Misha followed me, occasionally smelling about him and pissing on trees. Père Olivier had good skills in making and lighting campfires, it occurred to me. He brought cooked rations in his backpack instead of cooking on a fire – salted fish, cashew nuts, some fruit. My belly cried out for rice.

Animal noises then started, frightening me...and Misha, too. She lay her head on my lap. I took it and told her:

'Misha, you're supposed to protect us.' I watched as Père Olivier sucked a juicy plum till only the stone was left.

'How long more to Shanghai, Father?'

'Another day, I reckon.'

I asked him no more. I trusted his wisdom on so many things.

The fire crackled and ate our kindling wood. I placed a dead log on it. Père Olivier lay his head back on his backpack and closed his eyes. I could tell he was awake. Flying insects came down to the light of the fire and circled it. The night suddenly got chilly. I lay back with a blanket Li had packed for me and tried to rest, but animal howls and rustling in the trees prevented me. The whispering of the wind at night is more audible. As if it needs darkness to speak. Were these the spirits? And what about the Communists? I turned my eyes to face the stars but only saw darkness beyond the treetops. The dark sky with sparks and smoke swirling upwards towards it.

That night I watched as Père Olivier lay on his backpack. He had placed his hat to his side. He lay with his hands folded on his stomach, his eyes closed, but he never slept. Like a dog sleeps with one eye open, I thought. Then I noticed in his clasp, between his fingers, was the set of beads he kept, the ones he fingered in succession while muttering to himself.

When he had stopped I summoned up the courage to ask him:

'What is it you say to yourself, Father? When you speak in silence? What do you say?'

He opened his eyes calmly, considered this, and without looking at me, he smiled.

'I pray.'

'Pray?'

'I talk to God.'

God, I considered. This God he professed.

'What do you say?' To God?'

'But you can talk to Mary and to the holy saints also,' he said.

'I know so little,' I said.

'I know,' said Père Olivier. 'But you are willing.'

'I cannot force my faith on you as so many of my people have done before in order to save souls. It must be willing.'

'What do you say to God and these others?' I was wondering if they talked back to him.

'I tell them my needs, my concerns, and pray for others.'

'And,' he continued. 'There are set prayers we recite as well – like the *Pater Noster*, for example.'

'Pater nos...?' I made the sound.

'The Our Father – it's the Lord's prayer Jesus himself gave us.'

He lifted a twig and tossed it onto the crackling fire. Misha slept, her head resting on her paws facing the warm fire. I was puzzled.

'What does God say to you, then?'

Père Olivier grinned while staring at the night sky above. He thought for a while.

'He answers,' was his reply.

'I would like to learn to pray,' I said. 'This Jesus – the son,' I remembered, and said it.

'God the Son,' he said. 'God incarnate.'

'Is he powerful?' I asked, suddenly curious.

'Oh, yes.'

'Like Mao?'

Père Olivier laughed, 'Oh, yes,' he said.

'Are you a Communist?' I had to ask at last. 'Is Jesus the top Communist?'

Père Olivier rose on his side to face me.

'I am a priest of the Society of Jesus. Called Jesuits. I am a Jesuit priest.'

'What does that mean?'

'I bring the word of Jesus Christ to people who need it.'

'Like us, you mean?'

'Like you.'

'Our Order,' Père Olivier explained. 'Is sent to places where there is darkness, to bring light. We are called soldiers – soldiers of Christ. They call us the Pope's army.'

'The pope?' This word he used before to introduce himself to us.

'Is this pope a Communist?' I asked, thinking he had an army too, like Mao.

'The Pope is a Catholic.'

'And you?'

Père Olivier's blue eyes stared into my eyes, a sudden flash of light reflected. 'Yes,' he said.

I did not know what he meant then. Or even what I meant, about being Communist, Catholic. They were just words.

'What are you?' I asked.

'I am a Jesuit.' This word stuck in my head like so many other strange-sounding ones.

'Jesuit,' I repeated. 'Can I be a Jesuit?' I said.

The firewood crackled and burned and the black night sucked the smoke and sparks upwards. There was silence between us. Then Père Olivier spoke again:

'I have a sister, too.'

I looked at him, to hear what he would say.

'She is older than me, too', he said just staring into space.

I stopped feeding morsels to Misha and paid attention.

'She bosses me, *and*...she has boys...men chase her too.'

'Oh,' I said then. I wondered later why he told *me* this?

A white mist then covered the whole forest. A white puffy cloud – as if the skies above had descended on the trees. I heard a singing come from somewhere. Misha began to smell her way through the trees in the darkness. She smelled her way through the forest. I moved through the trees in the white mist but I wasn't walking, I was flying or floating. I floated onwards through wooded greenery like a ghost or spirit; one of the spirits that inhabit those woods above in the hills perhaps. Then, suddenly, Misha transformed into a serpent before me and wriggled along through the long grass and over stumps like a moving 'S'. On I followed, calling her back all the way. Then this serpent beckoned me. I came to an open area where a dozen men wearing hooded garments sat around a circular table. Some were *Laowai*.

I came to land right in the middle of the table. Beside me was a red coloured drink. One man reached in and gripped the cup and drank from it. The serpent plucked a fruit from a nearby bush using its fangs. It offered it to me. It looked like it was some kind of orange. Then another man appeared from nowhere. He, too, wore a hood. He fed me something white. I tasted it. I pulled his hood down. It was Père Olivier. He said, 'shush.' Then the first man spilled the drink over the table. It changed the whole table's colour to red. More men began pawing me all over till it tickled, all the while their eyes penetrated me with stares. The serpent spiralled over to me with the fruit, but I opted to eat the bread Père Olivier had given me. The white food that Père Olivier fed me made me feel light again, so I floated upwards to view the scene from above. It seemed so chaotic I could not look. Then I felt someone's tongue rough against my face. I opened my eyes. Misha was licking my face. A shrieking bat attacked us from out of nowhere. It was still dark. I had been dreaming. There was no white mist about anywhere and Père Olivier lay asleep across from us.

The Conversation

He was reading in the study room of the Residence. Jesuits lived mostly as communities and they had study rooms where the Fathers could read, reflect, and discuss. Books on religion, theology, all the philosophers from Plato to St Augustine to Marx, and all contextual, lined the shelves here. As was fitting for an Order renowned for scholars, no one book ever rested on a shelf long enough for dust to gather, although there always seemed to Jacques Olivier at any rate, a musty ambience about the place.

Over the big ornate fireplace hung a painting, apparently a clever copy from an Old Master. Around the walls hung saints, common biblical scenes and the Order's founder, St Ignatius, a standard on display in Jesuit communities. A simple crucifix hung over a shrine in a recess.

Olivier sat at a polished oak table at the end of the long room, reading a book.

The crystal doorknob twisted with a creak, the door opened, and in walked the Dean himself. Fr Kiely, his silver hair newly crew-cut, and a large white collar reminiscent of the head on a good pint of Guinness covered his athletic neck. Peter Kiely, an American Jesuit *obviously of Irish stock, jaunted about the room lightly touching the furniture and objects with the nimbleness of a wizard putting a spell on anything with his fingertips. He had a task to perform today, or a duty, perhaps – and it showed.*

'Well, Jacques, my man, you're at it again – the reading.'

Olivier's eyebrows lifted and he looked up in weary anticipation. As a teenager he had discovered how to show, or not, emotion by simple facial expressions, especially the eyebrows. His way of communicating nonverbally. A skill he had well honed in mirrors ever since.

'Yes,' Fr Kiely went on, the silence charming words out; not that he hadn't meant to speak anyway.

'Yes, my old grandmother used to say a little learning was no load to carry..'

'Quite,,' said Olivier.

'Quite, yes, quite, the company is renowned for it...study, learning. My own area is of course mathematics...' said Fr Kiely, using the Jesuits' own slang for the Order – the company.

'Quite.'

'And physics,' Fr Kiely added.

'Of that I am well aware, Father.'

'You trained in law, I understand?'

'Yes.'

All types, Father Kiely was thinking to himself...I wonder. He then glided around Olivier's seat till he was behind him. He peered down at Olivier's book.

'Let me see...aah, Milton...Paradise Lost.' Intriguing, thought Peter Kiely.

'You like Milton's story of Genesis, then?' he asked.

'I like the whole interpretation of the Genesis story, whether it is literal or metaphorical, you take from it what you will. For me it is explanatory.'

'The current thinking – since Darwin's discoveries – is that it's metaphorical, that it represents something.'

'The Fall of Man'

'Brought about by woman.'

'By the serpent.'

'And what or who was the serpent? Who does it represent?'

'According to Milton...and also our faith...Satan.'

'The Enemy.' Fr Kiely crossed himself and waited for Olivier to do the same.

'It is also foretold in the biblical version of the story, in Genesis, that woman, by crushing the head of the serpent, will save mankind at the end of days,' Olivier continued.

'Our salvation has been guaranteed by Calvary,' Fr Kiely said.

'The Gates of Hell shall not prevail, then?'

'Amen'

'Let us hope so,' said Père Olivier.

ext day towards evening we reached the summit of the last
hill. Clearing our way through the last of the brambles we
could look down the far side of it. And there they were; The
River once more, and on the other side was Shanghai itself...grey,
muggy, smoky, and it seemed noisy. Lights twinkling as one by
one they came on as evening closed in. The River poured its vast
waters all the way to Shanghai, and it seemed Shanghai sucked
The River's currents to it. The sea beyond, into which they
escaped, welcomed them, assimilating the muddy waters, not
exactly cohabiting but subsuming them. The incessant humming
of river and city orchestrated the oncoming night.

Père Olivier removed his hat and wiped his brow. I drank from
my water bottle. Without a word between us, we traipsed down
the slope. I did not tell Père Olivier about my dream or ask him
what it meant.

It was dusk when we crossed the bridge, and we suddenly found
ourselves there, in Shanghai. It surrounded us on all sides. Busy
streets like arteries, its people the blood; a heart thumping with
energy. Dogs yapped in the background. It seemed a disorganised
zoo. Coolies doing sprints along sidestreets, heaving of rickshaws
over wet, potholed dirt.

We were hungry. Père Olivier walked tall, his head above the others on the street, marched on, determined, leading the way. He never looked behind to check whether I, or indeed Misha, was following. He simply strode ahead. The aromas of food caught my senses. It smelled delicious. Where did it come from? I wanted to stop, look around me, take it all in, tired and all as I was, but Père Olivier's bobbing ginger head kept on moving like a float on a choppy sea of heads.

On each side street vendors called out – shoe repairs, ointments, tooth-pullers. I understood they were personally addressing me so I gesticulated back that I had no money. Some boys standing around laughed. Misha drooped along behind, head down at my heels. A few more streets and then I knew where Père Olivier was bringing us. I saw a huge canopy covering a sort of open-air eating house. Tasty fish was cooking on gigantic woks. I had never seen such woks. I wished Li could see – she would never believe me. Onions frying with chillies filled my nostrils. Père Olivier approached the vendor who was also the chef:

'How is Gingko?' he asked.

'He's okay. How you? Long time no see,' the small man said.

Père Olivier nodded, smiling his sore teeth smile again.

'Where can I find him?'

'Usual place.'

Père Olivier tipped the vendor with the currency, Golden Yuan, wherever he had found that, and saluted by tipping the brim of his hat. As we walked off the vendor shouted after:

'Bring him cigarettes. That's *his* currency – lots of ciggies! He's complaining about price of them.' Then he laughed and rattled a saucepan with his ladle for effect.

We went on till we came to another establishment. This time a tea house. A lone man was sitting outside at a table. Père Olivier went over to a skinny looking man wearing a cap, a cigarette between his teeth and chewing on something really fast so that it seemed he was having the cigarette for supper. I felt so hungry I would have eaten it.

'Go get some food,' Père Olivier said to me, handing me some currency. The man looked up with a skull-like countenance.

'Jacques, *mon ami,,*' he said warmly, his arms spread to embrace Père Olivier. They both hugged.

'Gingko, my old *compagnon. Comment est-il?*

Then they spoke in what I gathered was Père Olvier's own tongue for a bit. I went to order food. When I came back I sat away with Misha.

Père Olivier spoke low. Gingko too. Both sitting at the table, heads huddled together as if conspiring like two thieves. Gingko continuously topped up tea for them both from a pot-bellied teapot. Gingko smoked non-stop.

I sat away from them holding Misha and eating a spring roll stuffed with spring onion and bean sprouts. Misha licked the greasy ground. Overhead it looked grey, heavy with rain clouds.

It was pouring rain when we left Gingko, still smoking cigarettes while complaining about the price of them. Père Olivier had just given him a carton of *Lucky Strike*. Again I wondered where he had found these. Gingko said, 'Glad you didn't give me any cash. That new currency of theirs is useless...Golden Yuan? A fabrication to con us out of our gold! And inflation?', He lifted a carton. 'Know the price of this? They can't win this war with things like this.'

Although Asian, I got the impression Gingko was not a Chinese.

The rain lashed down on the streets causing the colourful city lights to reflect upwards from wet pools on the ground.

Shanghai! How I loved that word. How it fulfilled all my expectations. Père Olivier had got it out of Gingko that someone answering Johnny's description was downtown. I felt Li's letter tight under my shirt. We were, I felt, close to seeing him once again.

Johnny, who seemed so carefree – who was always full of talk and gossip that Li loved to hear, and always joking. That Johnny could have been such a different person behind it all. To be a soldier? To be prepared to kill? To have killed someone? Killed many, he said? The Johnny that Li said was too *nice*? Too nice for *her*.

But it is for our country, he said. Yet the others, those he went to kill are our countrymen, the Red Army, the Communists, they're ours, too. I thought to put this to Père Olivier to hear what he'd think.

Rain ran down gutters, flooding everywhere. We passed from narrow streets onto grander streets. Colours, flashing lights exploded everywhere about us. Could it be we were heading into Shanghai's 'Night-town'?

Infamous 'Night-town' was a place only of legend to us, brought to us by travellers passing through our village; a sort of place that me and Zhu would often talk about. In our dreams we'd have lists of wonderful things to do if we were ever there, all lustful!

About us people ran to escape the heavy rain, rickshaws scuttled past and across our path splashing water over us. My poor sandals were drenched wet. As soon as we reached the great streets motorcars appeared, honking noisily, beaming bright headlights through spraying rain. It got noisy.

We traipsed silently through the drizzled streets along the sidewalk, me and Misha in pursuit of Père Olivier, or so it would have seemed to any onlooker, just like when we were passing through the forest and the hills on our way to reach this huge city.

I had a head full of questions to put to the priest, such as how did he know his way around Shanghai? Was he here before? Who was Gingko   , and how did he know him? The question of where we were going was only the last on my inner-mind's list.

The neighbourhood quickly changed. Suddenly after turning from one street into another we came to bars and music and general mayhem. Club neon blinked different colours of light but all of them the darker hues of the rainbow – pinks, blues, and purples.

Père Olivier led us to one wide street. We stood outside a red door that looked almost part of the outside wall, it fitted so neatly. Pink bulbs flashed around it. Père Olivier told me to wait in the alley to the side of the building with Misha. It was an unlighted street. There I tied Misha to a lamppost with a light that didn't work. Père Olivier rapped three times on the door in a melodic pattern. Nothing happened at first, but eventually a slot opened and a pair of eyes gaped out on us. It was opened and we were admitted by two overgrown men wearing white tuxedos, smoking cigarettes. They slammed the door behind us. Père Olivier paid the men cash from the purse he carefully carried. The first man took the bank note, looked at it, and said, 'Look at this...not worth a damn pretty soon. Gold is God here!' He stared at Père Olivier. The other said mockingly, 'We'll never win this war at this rate.'

We were facing a stairway leading to what sounded like a place of enormous fun...music and chatter, I could hear. One of these men jerked his head to us to go up. At the top of the stairs was a curtain. We walked through.

Once inside, the lights suddenly dimmed. People were sat around tables eating, drinking, smoking. The aromas from the food were delicious. Then I saw them. How could I have missed them? They stood out so clearly *Laowai* – Western women! Looking so different from us. They were beautiful, I thought. Zhu would never believe this. The stories I would have for him when I returned. Who would have thought there was supposed to be a war on, or that this city was in danger of falling to the Communists? But then, I remembered, our village had not experienced the war till the Kuomintang marched in on that evening.

Women smoked long cigarettes, chatted with men both Western and Chinese. Sizzling trays of meats, potatoes, spring rolls, duck, and treats I never saw before or knew but smelled delicious, were carried by Chinese waiters to tables where sat Chinese, Americans, and Europeans, dressed in black suits and western bowties, white shirts.

And not only aromatic food drifted everywhere but smoke, too. Not just cigarette smoke but cigars and other herbal odours circulated the space. One of the first things I remember seeing was a girl selling cigarettes and cigars from a tray she carried as she walked about.

There was music; people danced on the floor to music I had never before heard. There was a band of musicians playing instruments I never saw before. And this music? It was so different from that of our village whenever someone would start to sing. Such life and vigour in it, this music. The men and women of all ages and castes danced around the floor surrounded by tables on an elevated level where all this delicious food was served.

I looked around for Père Olivier – he was nowhere to be seen so I went to search for him. I passed alongside walls of people, strangers, standing about holding drinks and smoking. Smells of perfume and cologne masking the food aromas.

I looked to the bar where drinks were served and saw something that caught my eye. I approached nearer this area to see better. People blocked my way standing in pairs or groups. I dodged them to get closer. And yes, I was sure of it – I saw him. Drinking alone at the bar...it was Johnny!...alone but surrounded by young women on either side. He appeared to be ignoring them, silently drinking. The women were tapping his shoulder and whispering in his ear and talking across him to each other.

I went to go over, my hand feeling for Li's letter in my tunic pocket. First I attempted to yell his name, but the noise of the club drowned my calls. A bartender looked curiously at me, thinking I was asking for a drink. Then Johnny looked over. His eyes met with mine...I think, for he appeared to be astonished at first. Then he looked again. Then he shook off the women and went to move in my direction.

'Get that into you, you look thirsty.' A glass with ice cubes and drink was slammed into my fist. In truth I felt so thirsty after the day, I thanked the gentleman. So I tasted the drink...ooh, so delicious. I drank it all down.

Suddenly the music tempo lifted. I heard it louder and clearer, then more squeaky sounds of laughter and voices. The crowd seemed to open up to allow me walk through. Everybody was open-gaped, laughing and smiling at me. Eyes shone and twinkled and enlarged. The colours got more blurred and confusing, changing constantly. I felt I was a lord.

I remember going to the dancefloor and tumbling around, holding hands with Western women. A man took me by the hand. I couldn't understand what he was saying. He led me to a table. He sounded familiar – the one who had given me the drink? Perhaps? Yes! Him!

'Here, son, come meet my friends'

Friends?

'All friends here,' a voice said. 'Good lad!' I felt a slap on my knee. 'Sit up here.' Another man patted a cushioned seat. He sounded Western, not Chinese...an American, maybe? I heard other strange languages spoken that night, too.

'You like another drink, kid?'

'Easy, don't kill the kid.'

'No, I meant a clean drink...no shit in it.'

I tasted another drink. It tasted strange. Very funny aftertaste. A sort of burning. I felt sick.

'Give him a smoke.'

'You dance pretty good, kid.'

'You like to come with us to another party?'

A dozen other strange voices and sounds filled my head. I looked upwards at a crystal globe glittering there above my head and I felt dizzy. My head ached and spun. Someone held me by the hand. I puked up on the table. Buff coloured puke full of diced spring onion and bean sprouts came out. The men's voices got louder, angrier...swear words...

Then, Père Olivier appeared dressed just as in my dream, holding his special bread. He gave the bread to me. I remember seeing this happen so very slowly. I recall every moment.

After Père Olivier, Johnny came. He hit one of the men and grabbed another by the collar.

Père Olivier took me and swung me up and away. Johnny hit another with a bottle, flinging the heavy ashtray at one other like a disc.

I was transported by Père Olivier behind the curtains and down the stairs again, passing the two white-suited men who were rushing up the stairs.

Next, I remember being outside a street café. Père Olivier and Johnny were by my side, each feeding me water from a cup while slapping my cheeks to rouse me.

'What is it? What's wrong with me?' I said.

'You've been drugged,' said Père Olivier.

'Yes, you are' Johnny said, the first time I heard his voice in weeks.

'Drugged?' I said. 'What do you mean?' I had, of course, heard about opium from the village's old people and all, but here I was puzzled.

'Slipped you a Mickey,' said Johnny.

'Johnny,' I said, and hugged him close. 'I have missed you.'

He was changed in appearance, in truth. More filled out in the face, stronger in the arms and body. He was unshaven.

'How are you here?' Johnny asked, looking around. Then I thought of it…Li's letter. Had I lost it? I felt my pocket. It was still there. I reached in, took it out, and handed it to him.

'It's from Li,' I said.

'I will not take,' he said.

'I think you should,' Père O spoke at last.

Johnny took the letter, opened it, and read.

'Where's Misha?' I asked Père Olivier.

'Where you left her,' he said. I felt concerned Misha would be taken.

'I'll get the old lady,' Père Olivier said and walked back the street. Johnny seemed confused.

'My uncle is unwell?'

'Lost a hand,' I told him.

'Shit!' He beat his leg with the letter. He was sobbing.

'We want you back, Johnny,' I said. I had heard his letters to Zhang being read out and I wanted Johnny to return so bad, to avoid the slaughter and madness he described.

'Who wants me? Li does not, certainly.'

'Johnny, *I* want you back.'

'I cannot.'

'Zhang-ze – he wants you.'

'He does? Why? To make his supper? To carry him home drunk? To listen to him talk bad of women and girls? To make me worse than I am?'

'He is wounded now.'

'All the worse for me.'

Then he stabbed his chest with, '*I* am wounded.'

A noise interrupted us. The sky went red in the west...an explosion.

'They are coming,' I said.

'So what?'

'Li wants you.'

'No! Li thinks I'm a fool. I, Johnny, am too *nice*! Too nice for *her*...for girls.'

'No...she wants you,' I said. 'She gave you a letter.'

'...That says my uncle is now an invalid and I must return now I am needed.'

Père Olivier then came holding Misha on the piece of rope. Misha walking tail down till she spotted me, then she went wild with excitement, licking and kissing me, her tail then moving like a fan.

'What's this?' Johnny said. 'A dog?'

'She's mine,' I said. 'Misha.'

Johnny bent and took Misha by the skull.

'She's a good one.'

'Yes,' I said.

'Good meat.'

'Do not speak that,' I said, hugging Misha.

Johnny smiled and winked.

'Survival makes us savages. *This* world is cruel.'

Johnny has changed, I thought then.

'Let us move,' said Père Olivier. 'We must leave the city by morning.'

'Yes, the sounds of the guns get nearer and nearer. They are surrounding us,' said Johnny.

'But you are not coming?' I said.

'We must return through the hills and uplands. The river will be blockaded,' Johnny said.

'The way we came?' I said.

'Exactly, an army doesn't make much progress marching through a forest. But we can'

'You are coming, then?'

'Out of Shanghai, yes. There's nothing left for me here. We will see where to.'

As we walked along the dark, deserted streets of Shanghai at midnight, the sky to our west lit up bright. Noise of cannons exploding somewhere not far away thundered.

A checkpoint of soldiers guarded the way out.

'Papers, please.'

'Christian Missionary,' said Père Olivier, showing the guards some document.

The soldier examined the paper, turning it upside down and sideways.

'And these?' He asked, indicating me and Johnny.

'The designated guides to my region,' said Père Olivier.

The soldiers looked us up and down with suspicion, then eyed Misha.

'What do you think?' one asked the other.

'Let them out of here. Only fools go that direction. The Reds will kill them for sure – a missionary? Let him pull that on *them*!'

'Pass,' the young soldier said.

We left Shanghai with what we had come for. We headed towards the uplands to take us back home.

We reached those hills again, and the forest. Walking in file, Père Olivier first, then Johnny, then me, then Misha, we encountered those same obstacles; fallen boughs, trunks, mounds of earth, rocks, which helped lengthen our journey.

Nights we slept around a small campfire. We had used up our rations, me and Père Olivier, so we foraged, eating on the go. Johnny was good here. He snared us a hare and some squirrels. I missed my rice so much my belly ached.

Around dusk one night Père Olivier set about making a fire. He instructed me to go search for wood, preferably dead wood, for burning as well as twigs. I took Misha to explore a section of the forest over to one side. Johnny had caught something in a snare for us to eat and was already skinning it.

I went along into the forest, gathering logs, and when my arms could no longer carry the load, I would return to deposit them at our camp, then back again – you can never have enough firewood.

It began to get darker when I reached a clearing in the forest. Surrounding this clearing around the edges where it bordered the high trees, there was plenty of deadwood I could use. I began to slowly pick them up. Misha was, as usual, sniffing about, leaving her mark. The various noises in the forest got quieter now; a dead calmness fell about the place. I sat on my hunkers momentarily, looking about me, contemplating. My view was serene, lush grass, dark green forest on all sides. Nature's noise in the background. All in the balmy evening's twilight. I wondered what old Zhang's Lao Tzu would have to say about this scene or even if I could come out with my own wisdom. Père Olivier would only refer to Christian scripture I suppose, something profound.

Then I heard a scuffling sound, a sort of scraping over the far side directly opposite me. A couple of wild birds flew up from the bushes. Misha stopped scratching around and looked attentive, her trained ears tweaked to listen. The bushes stirred gently as if a gust of wind had blown them. Branches shook slightly.

Footsteps? I tensed where I was squatting down. The crack of twigs under feet...then I saw it. It came aimlessly into the clearing, with light brown hair and dappled white spots – a deer, and a young one at that. It leapt over a fallen bough and into the grass. It stood awkward – its long legs looking like its body hadn't yet grown to fit them.

Misha sat down and tilted her head; she had never seen a deer before. Her nostrils were working overtime. The young deer seemed to be lost, puzzling where next to go. Suddenly it froze. It had smelled us. It stood there legs apart when our eyes met. It blinked. Misha approached it, but it didn't run away. When Misha got up front she sniffed the young deer's hooves. Then she playfully offered the paw. The deer then smelled Misha's paw, then stomped its hoof in a playful gesture. This pawing and hoofing play went on a bit. The deer then looked behind Misha towards me as if it had picked up my scent. Its nose twitched at the air, and its eyes, brown, moist, innocent eyes, met mine. For a fleeting instant, I thought, there was a trust, an understanding. I stood up so it could see properly that I meant no harm. I could see it taking this in, calculating, wondering. Then it backed away from Misha and, in a couple of skips, it was gone another direction back into the green forest.

When I eventually returned to the campsite, Père Olivier and Johnny were roasting a squirrel. I never told them what I saw. I just thought about praying to Père Olivier's God for that young deer that night.

Before we slept Johnny asked us:

'How did you know where I was – in Shanghai?'

'Père Jacques here knew,' I said.

'How?' he asked, looking at Père Olivier.

Père Olivier finished gnawing on a bone, wiped his hands, and answered, 'I have some contacts.'

'How? Who?' said Johnny, looking concerned.

'I was a missionary in Shanghai before I came to Zhaoui,'he said.

'So?'

'I fed the poor. It can be advantageous to know the streets...and street-dwellers.'

'Gingko?' I said.

'One of my contacts,' said Père Olivier.

'And?'

'Gingko is useful...at times,' Père Olivier smiled, thinking to himself.

'He's Chinese?'

'Vietnamese,' said Père Olivier. 'A good Vietnamese.'

'And how did he hear of me?' Johnny asked.

'From how I described you,' said Père Olivier.

'How?'

'I described how you looked.'

'In a city like Shanghai, how could he know who I was and where I was?'

'He didn't, exactly. We guessed...we were lucky. He knew you were drinking. That is the only nightclub still open in Shanghai now. Shanghai is in its final days now just like Babylon before the fall.'

'And how did you describe me?'

'A wide-eyed country lad, who smells of fish and who walks with a smile.'

Johnny said nothing more; he went quiet again.

'Providence,' said Père Olivier. 'It was providence.'

BOOK

II

The flag blew in the light May breeze, scarlet crimson, emblazoned with hammer and sickle symbols, but the wind wasn't strong enough to keep it going, so it became limp and just fluttered about the top of the mast.

No matter what business passers-by were doing, they had to stop and stand rigid while two Red Army soldiers hoisted the flag up the mast. This was each morning.

Having stood at attention while this brief ceremony went on we went about our chores again.

I joined a line to get fish. Just one big one and a small one were doled out to me by Lao, who was watched by a Red Army soldier. Other villagers were behind me in the queue. Li was also in a line – for rice and vegetables.

Fishing still happened on The River but the Red Army took all the catch, and after taking their portion, the remainder was distributed among the village. It was free but allocated according to what was deemed appropriate to each house. This rule Tang brought in.

The villagers thought much of this; free food. It was a big thing to see who got what.

'How did you do?'

'Three carp.'

'Three?'

'Yes, you?'

'Four crayfish.'

'Only four? How many do you have at home?'

'Wait till the line for rice,' another joked.

'I miss all the haggling,' a woman said.

One old man grumbled, 'I'm going to complain to Mayor Xi.'

'Xi?' Another said, 'Sure, he's under lock and key.'

'No, he's not!'

'Yes, he's relieved of his duties – '

'Duties.'

'Whatever they were. And ordered not to leave his house.'

'But Mister Wu still sells in *his* store?'

'He might well run the store now, but he doesn't sell. Selling is forbidden now.'

'Who is in charge now?'

'Tang.'

'Him?'

'No, the committee is.'

'Yes, and the committee elected Tang.'

I walked on. Li was to form a line for rice and vegetables.

I called to see Zhang-ze. Misha followed me. Old Zhang was visited daily now by the army medic attached to the Red Army Company that occupied the village. Tang was the commander, elected by the men. Only two ranks were permitted: Private and Commander. A Commander had to be elected by the men.

'We abhor rank,' Tang explained. '...and hierarchy. Things are more democratic now.' Tang even set up a committee to run Zhaoui after he dismissed Mister Xi as mayor. Tang served on this, as did Johnny, who was chosen to represent fishermen.

'Well, Zhang, how are you keeping today?'

'Bah!'

He was drinking wine from a cup in his good hand, his right having a bandaged stump at the end. He drank all the time now. He lifted his cup to me.

'At least my hand mobility is the same direction our country is taking,' he said.

'How so?'

'Left...but it doesn't work for long,' he laughed.

'Lao Tzu?' I wondered.

'Bah!' he spat, and gestured me to leave. 'I am truly cursed.'

Père O was allowed to stay in his hut to the rear of the long shack he used as his 'Parish Church'. The church was now used to billet the soldiers.

I decided to call on him. Two guards were posted at his door watching everyone who called on him. He was not allowed out till it was decided what to do with him, him being a *Laowai* and all.

When we returned to the village that time from Shanghai after travelling through those hills again, it was dusk. A red globe of sun descended over the hill to the west, making an orange hue mixed with the grey of approaching night. The street was quiet. The village dogs made a barking fuss when we came on the deserted street. Misha crept along behind me.

We would go straight to Zhang with Johnny. It *was* possible Li would be there tending to him. True, Zhang did not like women, but Li could bully him into liking her.

Old Zhang was bent over the table, his back to the door. A lighted candle was in the middle of the table and some empty rice wine bottles. He held a cup in his left hand and the stump was bandaged. Someone had tended to it properly, it looked like.

'Uncle Zhang,' said Johnny.

A pair of bleary eyes turned to look behind, bloodshot.

'Oh...it's you.'

We looked at each other. *This* was a welcome?

'How are you, Uncle?'

Old Zhang raised his right arm, showing his bandaged stump where his hand had once grown.

'I heard what happened.'

'Bah! My ill luck again.'

Johnny seemed shy or embarrassed by this statement. He glanced to see did I or Père O note it.

Then Père O said, 'You have been looked after, Zhang-ze. 'He nodded at the bandage.

Zhang lifted his cup with his left hand. 'Not really.'

It was empty.

'Let me fill it, Uncle Zhang.' Johnny reached for a bottle – but it was empty, too – only drops came out. Then another. Finally, a third – all empty.

'There's nothing left.'

'Are you eating well, Zhang-ze?' Père O asked.

Sad, moist, bloodshot eyes in a hairy grey-stubbled face nodded. He blubbed, 'Aa-haah.'

'Li? How is Li?' Johnny asked then.

Zhang shook his head.

'The person who bandaged your hand?' Père O said, looking over Zhang's shoulder. I sensed something was up when he said that.

Then I heard a click. The front door had opened, and when we turned round to look, there stood Tang with two soldiers wearing olive green tunics with a red square emblazoned on their collars – Communists!

I had finally come face-to-face with the feared Communists. I had, in a way, always anticipated this moment. Tang and his Company of Red Army soldiers were in Zhaoui at last.

A rifle was aimed at Johnny and Père Olivier, while Tang held a hand gun.

'Welcome home, gentlemen,' he said. 'We've been waiting.'

'Comrade Tang.' Pere Olivier nodded with respect.

'What is this?' demanded Johnny. 'Who are you?'

'Hello, Johnny,' said Tang. 'You don't remember me?

'You used to follow us as a kid and copy the games we played.'

Johnny tried to focus his eyes on Tang, blinking them a few times.

'Tang – it's you! You left the village to fight the Japs.'

'And you left to fight us.'

'You are a Communist?'

'I am Commander Tang of 'B' Company, Jiangsu Division, People's' Liberation Army, and we've liberated this village in the name of the People's' Republic.'

'Two days ago,' said old Zhang. 'That's when they came.'

'Where's Li?' said Père O.

'Yes,' said Johnny. 'Where is she?'

Tang lifted an eye:

'You are concerned for Li?' he asked suspiciously.

'Naturally,' said Père O.

'I was speaking to Johnny.'

'Her young brother is here,' Johnny said, grabbing at my shoulders.

Tang looked at me. I feared Tang. Ever since I could remember him, I feared him.

'Li is waiting for you at home,' he said. He opened the door for me and I ran.

'But why did you leave them there alone?' Li shouted at me, vexed or frustrated.

'I thought...'

'You thought! You know what "thought" did?'

'But Johnny lives there, it's his home!'

'And Père Olivier?'

'What of him?'

Li stayed cautious and did not answer. Since when did she care about Père O?

'What will Tang do?' I said then.

Li pushed her hair back, not answering.

'I'm scared of Tang,' I said.

All of this happened two weeks ago now. It is said you always meet your deepest fears. That's why you should never articulate them, for they will surely come. I had lived in fear of the Communists – because I did not understand them perhaps. But now we lived among them, with them, under them. And life was normal.

Because Johnny had returned, I was no longer needed to fish The River for Zhang. Johnny and Lao did the fishing with the other village fishermen. Zhang stayed in his house now, drinking. This was obvious, for he could be heard swearing to himself and sometimes his voice would carry singing rude songs. On occasions he would walk along the riverbank watching for Johnny's boat and give a hand offloading the catch – 'a one-handed hand' as Lao joked to me.

The landed catch of all the fishermen was piled together and some soldiers would weigh the catch or count the fish, depending if it were a good day or a bad one, then note it down. Another soldier who called himself a 'quartermaster' then took a full net for the army. The remainder was distributed to the villagers who made a line daily to receive their quota. Johnny and Lao did the handing out. Johnny was elected to represent fishermen on a Committee that oversaw the village in place of Mayor Xi and the

Elders. Johnny's job was to make a list of the amounts of fish to give each house. Some days there would be very little, just minnows and whelk and the like, but Johnny was always generous to me, and indeed, to those he favoured.

It was similar for the vegetables, and rice came in canvas sacks to the general store run by Mister Wu. The delivery was every week. The committee, run by Tang, ordered the rice to be free as well, 'equal distribution' he called it. But I overheard Mister Wu grumbling:

'At this rate I can't afford to bring rice in if I don't make a profit by selling it.'

'It is equal distribution now, Wu,' Tang told him. 'Food for all.'

'Equality is fine,' said Mister Wu, 'but I am not treated equal.'

'How so?'

'Well, I can't make profit, so I suffer...and rice is getting scarce, I'll have you know.'

'Do you want the whole village to suffer because of your needs?'

'Look, I am in business; if everyone across the board gives and takes for free, well, and good, but it's not fair, I am paying to order rice and you order me to give it free. Let the whole country go socialist first then we can have equality. But it's not. Now you want socialism here in Zhaoui but in outside parts people still have commerce. I am all for equality but I'm no fool.'

'We will discuss this at the next committee meeting, Wu,' said Tang.

Other foodstuffs like caught game – hares or pigeons – insects, and wildlife hunted were permitted as usual, provided they were bartered if the hunters didn't want to eat them themselves. Money was no longer used – the Gold Yuan of the Republic belonged to the old regime of Nationalist China. The Communists controlled this region now although the war carried on in other parts Very little news now came to the village. Travel was considered dangerous.

I went on playing with Zhu and Misha. We went exploring the countryside around. The hills that once fascinated and frightened me no longer did. And I didn't feel there was anybody watching me from above anymore. Except the golden sun that got warmer – it was now mid-May and summer was coming.

Myself and Zhu carried on, now accompanied by Misha. One day as we walked along the riverbank we saw Pere O. He was reading his book, walking slowly. A soldier was shadowing him, walking a few paces behind. We went over to him.

'Hello, Father.'

He glanced up from his book.

'Hello. What are you up to?'

'Just out walking,' we answered, looking over his shoulder at the soldier. 'That's all.'

'I am allowed out now. The summer is coming so I can't very well be indoors all the time...Commander Tang has...' He looked at the guard. '...has allowed me outdoors now.'

'Oh.'

'Yes,' he said, with a jerk of the head to indicate the soldier, With an escort.'

The soldier must have seen us look over, for he jabbed his rifle and barked:

'No talking here. You...move. Move on.'

Misha had by now gotten used to Père O and treated him as part of the pack. She growled, showing fangs at the guard. The guard lifted his rifle like a club to threaten Misha, so we walked away.

We left Père O standing there reading from his black leather book, with his guard standing around seeming bored.

'There's that fat dog again.'

'Yes, I see. She'll make good supper.'

I looked around. It was Chen and Lee, two village youths, who were a bit older than me and Zhu. I always remembered them as up to no good. Now, all of a sudden, they had grown up. They were always together and could be trouble. Mister Wu used to chase them from his store because they never bought anything when they went in.

Me and Zhu walked fast to get by them. Then Chen, who was fat and mean, stood in our way.

'Why rush off?'

We both stood there dumb, thinking of what we could say.

'We must go,' said Zhu in a panicky voice. My mother is expecting us.'

'Your mother?' said Chen, looking over our shoulders at Lee, who was standing behind us.

'Your mother?'

'And *your* mother?' he looked at me. I did not answer. I reddened when he said that. He caught this. Mother was dead.

'Ooh...you have none,' he said, grinning slyly like a dead hare. 'No Mama...boo hoo,' he laughed teasingly. Lee sniggered.

'We must go,' I said, walking on. Misha then growled, sensing something wrong. Chen didn't like it. Lee stood back afraid.

'That dog is vicious,' Chen said. 'It ought to be killed.'

'Come on, Zhu,' I said.

'Wait! Why move away? We can show you something that will amaze you.'

He walked in front of our path again. I gripped Misha tight.

'You.' He pointed at Zhu. 'You can show it to your mother. She will love it.'

'We must go now,' said Zhu.

I gripped Misha by the scruff of the neck. She was snarling at Chen.

'No,' said Chen. 'We have found a beautiful bird's nest with eggs that are so rare. The colours? Such colours...green and black and brown and yellow.'

'Where?' said Zhu.

'Come,' Chen said, and he walked on ahead. I looked at Zhu, then we both followed. I did not want or need to see this birdnest, and I doubt Zhu did either, but at least we were walking now and heading back towards the village.

Chen led the way towards the stream that ran alongside the village behind the houses. Flowers were in bloom everywhere. Lee followed us along. We walked beside the tinkling stream for a bit, then Chen hopped across it and we all had to follow, balancing on stones so as not to get wet.

They brought us to an area of wild bush in flower with tall grass stems surrounding it. Sweet smells everywhere.

'In here,' Chen said, ushering us into a gap in the bush. I immediately sensed something not right but walked in anyhow, so did Zhu. I ordered Misha to sit outside. Inside the circular space, Chen grabbed my bamboo stick while Lee stood at the entrance.

'Where are the eggs?' said Zhu, getting anxious. Lee let out a laugh. I felt my heart thumping. Chen and Lee were bigger than us.

'Now, lads,' said Chen, smiling with some teeth going black. 'Show us your arses and we will let you go.'

Lee snorted a snigger at this. Chen tapped the palm of his left hand with the bamboo while grinning. I heard Zhu sighing, stifling quiet sobs. I looked around me. Tall bush surrounded us on all sides except the gap where Lee stood. I do not know what made me think of it, but I said: 'Misha is sick. I can hear her.'

'Show us your arse first,' said Chen.

I backed back towards the gap. I could see Zhu getting very scared and agitated.

'What is it?' demanded Chen.

'It's Misha,' I said. 'I can hear her.'

'Misha is dogfood,' he snapped.

'She is sick. I hear her.'

Lee looked confused, looking at Chen for an order.

'Show us your arses,' said Chen. 'Then we let you go.'

'I think I'm going to be sick, too,' I said, turning towards Lee. I pretended to puke in front of Lee. He hopped out of my way like his feet were on fire, leaving the gap clear.

'Now, Zhu,' I shouted. 'Run!'

I skipped through the small gap and ran as fast as I could. Misha followed. I ran and ran. I could hear the ground pounding under my feet. Sensing something behind me, I turned to look back at one stage. I could see Zhu running another direction, but just behind me, on my heels, was Chen, reaching out to grab me, the bamboo stick in his other hand. I ran even faster. Chen's arm stretched to grab hold of me when we came to the stream. I gave the mother of all leaps and cleared the narrow gushing stream in a single jump. Then I heard splashing. I looked. Chen had either tripped on a stone or slipped on the wet rocks of the stream, for he had landed in the gushing, fast-flowing water. Misha let out a volley of barks with the excitement. I ran all the way home with Misha. I could hear Chen shouting behind us.

'I'll get you...one day. I will get you. And I'll have your miserable dog for supper.'

Li, who I already said could read, was now brave enough to do it in public. Tang had said all women were now equal to men. Old Zhang took this news so badly he joined the queue for fish one day. A lady named Fang tapped his shoulder:

'Zhang-ze, what are you doing in line? Doesn't your nephew bring fish?'

'I am doing what you are doing, Ma'am, he said.

'But you have Johnny to bring fish.'

'What are *you* doing here?' Zhang said.

'Queuing for fish,' she said.

'Me too. We are all equal now.'

'But households are only allotted a quota each. It's not for individuals.'

'Individualism is banned now,' said another.

'And women run the household now?' said Zhang.

'Yes, Zhang-ze,' she said. 'I do.'

'I have no woman to run mine.'

'But you can get fish,' she said.

'Johnny works. Do you?'

'I can see,' the woman laughed. 'You clearly don't work anymore!' and she mimicked some gesture with her hand I didn't understand. Not then anyway. Everyone laughed.

'Bah!' said Zhang. 'Women are now more equal than men, I can see.'

Before, village women did not read, not publicly, anyhow. They were not schooled in reading or encouraged to. Any woman who did was treated with suspicion. I never asked Li how she learned to read, but she was always clever. I was, however, curious to know where she got the books she now read. Once, I examined closely the words written on the covers:

Communist Manifesto, Karl Marx

Engels on Marx, Friedrich Engels

On Guerrilla Warfare, Mao Tse-tung

Then again, underneath the pile, there it was again, *'Holy Catechism of the Catholic Church'*, and another under that, *Paradise Lost.*

I asked Li one day about her reading.

'What do you read, Li? What stories are in those books?'

Li laughed. 'Stories?'

'Yes. Are the books funny or interesting?'

She considered the question.

'Interesting, certainly,' she said.

'Tell me something from them.'

'They are political, the books. About the revolution going on – in our country...and outside.'

'Revolution?'

'Yes, the old order is dying and a revolution is happening – led by Comrade Mao. The old world order is in decline also. This has been foretold by Marx.'

I did not understand all she was saying, so I said:

'What about Comrade Tang?'

'Tang is leading the revolution here – in Zhaoui. Appointed by Mao Tse-tung himself, he was.'

'Tang here, Mao China, Marx the world?'

Li laughed at this. 'Yes, sort of,'   she said.

I was shy about mentioning Père O and his teaching me from one of the books I saw her with, so I said out of curiosity:

'What else do you read?

She turned. 'What do you mean?'

'Who gives you the books?' I said then.

'Tang,' she answered quickly. 'Tang lets me read his books.'

'About revolution?'

'Yes, why?

'No why.'

I wanted to learn more about what she knew about Père O and his faith. I wandered seemingly aimlessly past the pile on the table.

'And what is this one?' I plucked up the last book left there. Li took it from me, and screwing her eyes to read it, said:

'Aah, this is a long poem that tells a funny story.'

'A story? Tell me.'

'I am not finished with it yet. It is difficult.'

'A poem that's also a funny story?'

Li sighed, as if tired of my questions. She sat on the bench looking at the book. She opened it and read:

"Of Man's first disobedience and the fruit Of that forbidden tree whose mortal taste Brought death into the world and all our woe..."

Then she said, 'It is a belief of some faiths that once – many, many years ago – our ancestors lived in a paradise. They had everything they wanted – fruit, fresh flowers, waterfalls – Earth's bounty. A beautiful garden given to them by God. But one day a snake found the woman alone and tempted her to taste a certain fruit in this garden, a fruit that God told them strictly never to eat. But the snake said if she tasted it she would become like God. So she ate the forbidden fruit. Then she got the man to eat it. When God found out, he was very angry and expelled them, man and woman, from this garden paradise.'

'That *is* a funny story,' I said. 'A talking snake!'

'Yes,' said Li, concentrating. 'But the snake was really a powerful demon in disguise.'

'How so?'

'You see there are demons...and evil spirits...as well as good ones.'

'You believe in this?'

'I believe human beings can be tempted,' she said.

'To do evil?'

'Yes,' she said.

'Where did they go then? The man and woman.'

'Here. To this world, where there is evil and death.'

'When was this?' I asked.

'Many, many years ago. To our first ancestors.'

'It is funny that it was the woman who tempted the man,' I said. 'I can see this every day in the village. And just look at how Johnny behaved with you,' I joked.

Li turned and snapped at me. 'Don't say that!'

I fell quiet then, but had to ask her, 'Why then did the snake first tempt the woman, not the man?'

Li looked up then away again.

'And how did this snake manage to tempt her, the woman? What sweet words did it use?' I laughed. Li looked at me awkwardly; she did not say anything.

'What does this mean?' I said after a while.

'I am not sure,' she said. 'I only know that we are always...sometimes, I mean, tempted.'

'Are you, Li?' I asked. 'Tempted to do evil and wrong?'

She stayed quiet again.

'How can we trust people, then, Li?'

She considered this for a while, then rubbing her clenched fingers across her forehead, said,

'Sometimes I'm not sure if I even trust myself.'

'It is easy for a girl to fall in love,' she went on. 'For even as children we played with dolls and dreamed of love while boys fished and fought with each other.'

I listened and I truly did not understand the grown up world I realised. So I went out to play with Misha. Li remained there staring into space.

I have heard it said since that in certain places – prisons, mental hospitals, reform schools – cigarettes, tobacco are currency. That could be the way it was amongst a few in Zhaoui at that time as well. We could only barter so much – equivalent exchange was what Tang's committee called it. Food was free. So, for some items trade was with tobacco. Most people smoked. I have also heard it said tobacco is a drug and highly addictive. This must be true, for I have myself seen old Zhang smoke dried tea leaves when he could not find any cigarettes.

Trade with the outside became scarce, and when it did it was expensive; this war brought about shortages for sure.

There was, however, no longer a shortage of men in the village. The Red Army at first maintained a distance from the villagers. Unlike the Kuomintang who billeted in the long shack used by Père O as a church, the Red Army pitched canvas tents near the entrance to the village from the west, the same road Père O had appeared from a few months before.

But, over time they began to mix with the girls. Tang had informed us it was fundamentally an army of the people – 'a Peoples' Army for a People's' Republic'.

Some of the girls clapped when he said this, but most villagers looked confused. They did not in truth bother or really care for politics. Mayor Xi and his family had always been Elders and in business in the village, even when the Kuomintang came to power.

Tang, when younger, was alleged to be a 'firebrand'. He had proven his commitment to his principles by returning to the village as head of a 'people's' army'.

Li, I knew, also understood politics but was skilful in keeping her thoughts to herself. She could read books. Her strong opinions, though, often escaped.

Old Zhang was the only other I ever heard mention politics, usually with a lot of swearing. He knew a thing or two, I suspected, and often muttered political slogans to himself.

Many times I heard the other old men nod towards him and speak under their breath that old Zhang had in his youth also been a firebrand. But now it was all Lao Tzu with him. I often thought what it must have been like those years ago, what sayings or beliefs did he spout. Did they have the same type of wisdom then as now?

Human nature, I have learned, is disposed to breaking rules rather than obeying them. Some rules anyway. Tell someone they mustn't do something and sooner or later they will do that thing. Otherwise the urge gets stronger and stronger, till you eventually capitulate.

This is especially true with sexual mores.

Though ordered to remain in his house by Tang, Père O could now receive visits. This was mostly intended for food delivery. I had been trying to read the books Père O gave me before Tang liberated us and took over the village. They were difficult to make sense of, written in Mandarin, but I remained curious about the faith Père O professed and preached, so I volunteered to bring him his food ration. Like all rules strictly laid down at first, the house arrest of Père O was getting lax and the guards fed up. Already he was allowed outdoors to walk the riverbank with a soldier to watch. Now, each time I brought his food, I could enter the house for half an hour each day. The guard who seemed endlessly bored never questioned this.

Once inside, Père O gave me instructions in his faith and answered any questions I had on the matter. In truth I was confused by all the beliefs I was encountering of late and needed certainty. With Li reading Marx, Tang's Mao, Zhang with Lao Tzu, what next, I wondered?

It was during one particular meeting, Père O was describing to me his God's Ten Commandments, that I made my thoughts known. At first I felt much excitement to learn about God's rules for mankind – what it all meant, or was meant to be. Père O went on reading these:

"Thou shalt not steal... Thou shalt not kill... Thou shalt not commit adultery..."

It was all, "Thou shall not do this and thou shall not do that!" I had to interrupt Père O with:

'Why is it God always saying not to do such and such?

He looked at me.

'We all sin...I do,' he said, pleading with his eyes.

'You, Father?'

'Yes,' he exclaimed. 'Even me.'

'You do, too, no doubt,' he said then.

I blushed when he said this. He noticed, I am sure. I felt ashamed then, thinking he knew.

'But why does he not tell us to do such and such? I mean, Father, how to live instead of how not to live?' I blurted out quickly.

Père O seemed puzzled when I said this. He said nothing at first, then flicked to a page in his big book, his Bible.

'Here,' he said, through spectacles on the end of his long nose:

'*"Love one another"*, and here...' He continued flicking to yet another page. '*"...You must love thy neighbour as thyself"*

I listened to this.

'But I do not love my neighbour, Father, or anybody else – most people, I mean.'

'You love Li, don't you?'

'Yes, Father...and Misha.'

Père O waved his hand when I said Misha, as if that was not what he meant. He took off his glasses.

'It is hard, I admit. But it's all for a reason,' he said. 'You see, in the afterlife, or Heaven if you like, there is no place for hatred or disliking anybody there. You cannot enter Paradise, the Kingdom of God, and hate people...other souls who are there. It is all love.'

'Why, then, are all God's Commandments telling us what not to do, not what to do?'

'But I gave an example where he tells us to do something – to love.'

'But that's Jesus, not God.'

Père O looked annoyed. 'Jesus *is* God,' he said. 'He is God the Son. Then there is God the Father *and* God the Holy Ghost, the so-called Holy Trinity consubstantial, with each other.'

'Con –sub – stant...?' That word I had heard him say before.

'Then God the Father's rules are all saying do not do something.'

'You think this?' he said, perplexed.

'Yes, Lao Tzu is different,' I said.

He seemed grave behind it all. There was an easygoing demeanour, which could be intense, but he acted as if he understood and accounted for all our human failings, as if he had to put up with us. As if the world was a horrible place and *he* knew that and could not change it. But his frowning now worried me. Was I in danger of being lost? Damned, as he once called it?

'Père O then fingered through his Bible again and read aloud:

"And the Lord God commanded the man, 'You are free to eat from any tree in the garden; but you must not eat from the tree of the knowledge of good and evil, for when you eat from it you will certainly die."

Then he closed the book and took his spectacles off to chew the ends, pondering some matter.

'You can go now,' he told me. 'I need to rest some.'

As I made my way to the door, I saw him reach for the book I spotted at home, the one Li spoke about, the funny story about the talking snake, the book called *Paradise Lost.* I hoped then that my words did not mean I had lost going there, to paradise. I also hoped   I hadn't offended Père O himself. For it struck me he was the type of man who had to struggle to be relaxed in company, with his tight lips and tense smiles and head nods. He needed to trust fully those around him in order to relax.

Whenever I thought of suffering thereafter, I thought of Misha; how innocent she was, relying only on my good nature, on man's good nature. So trusting and so loyal. This world seems abundantly fruitful, yet also a repository of suffering – animal suffering, man suffering. No matter how much we accumulate we must always suffer. Why was this, I wondered?

Outside the two guards were tossing some cards onto the ground, playing some game. They were truly bored, I thought.

Then one day I brought two seatrout home for supper. When I handed them to Li I noticed she sniffed at them, making an ugly face.

'But, Li, it's fresh.'

'Johnny?'

'Yes, Johnny gave me them' – there were two trout. She took them and her demeanour looked ill.

'Are you alright, Li?' I said.

She turned. 'Yes, of course I am.'

'You look sick,' I said.

'I better not eat fish, so,' she said, turning her back to me.

I was so delighted when she said this.

'Can I have two, then, Li?'

'I guess,' her back answered. She still faced away from me.

I could not believe I was hearing this – two trout? And Li, who loved seatrout, refusing to eat hers? Truly I felt blessed.

At table that evening I prayed a silent prayer in thanks for the food. Li watched me.

'What are you doing? Eat,' she gestured.

'I'm saying a prayer.'

'A what?'

'A prayer...in thanks for this food.'

Li looked annoyed.

'These are two good fried trout in front of you and you pause to pray? I thought you would devour them?'

'It was Père Olivier who told me to offer thanksgiving for food,' I said.

'What did he say?'

She was always curious about Père Olivier and his words, I felt.

'To give thanks for food we receive – God's bounty he called it.'

When I finished my little prayer I ate my fish fast. Li simply picked at her bowl of rice.

'What is it, Li? Are you not hungry, Li?'

'I don't know,' she said. 'Maybe not.'

I eyed the bowl of rice greedily.

'May I eat it?' I asked.

Li looked at me.

'No!' She slammed her chopsticks on the table and removed the rice bowl.

'You get two fish and now you want extra rice. You are too greedy, that's what.'

'You complain I don't eat. Now it's you who won't eat! You don't touch your food...I just thought...' I said.

'Thought? You know what thought did?' she said.

'Anyway, we must save our rice now,' she went on. 'There are shortages.'

'How so?'

'Mister Wu says he cannot get supplies – for now at least – due to the war.'

I placed my bowl of rice aside when I heard this. Li spotted it.

'You ask why I don't eat, now you are not hungry?' she said.

I just shrugged without speaking; Li could be very sharp and perceptive.

'You don't want it?'

'Yes, but I have just eaten two large fish – trout – two good ones!'

Li seemed interested. You could not fool with her, I knew. She rested her head in her palms, elbows on the table, and smiled.

'Alright,' I said. 'It's for Misha.'

'That dog?'

'She's mine,' I said 'I must feed her.'

'With good rice?'

'What else?'

'It will get scarce, rice. You cannot give your good food to animals.'

'She's mine. My family,' I said louder.

Li placed her forearm on the table and tapped with her fingers. She was considering what to say next. She spoke slowly:

'You must take Misha into the forest and lose her,' she said calmly. I could not believe it. What was Li saying?

'No,' I said. There were tears from my eyes now.

'Yes,' she said. 'If you love her you must.'

'But Li?'

'I can't say anymore,' she said quietly, under her breath. She stood up, taking her plate away.

'Why are you not eating, Li?' I said.

'I'm not hungry.'

I went outside to visit Misha, who was tied up out the back yard. When I appeared she stood wagging her tail, covering my hands with her licks.

'Here, Misha, good girl.' I had brought the bowl of rice I hadn't eaten with me. I emptied it on the ground. Misha lapped it all up in seconds.

'Good girl,' I said.

'I will not let anything happen to you, Misha – ever!'

The noise we used to hear of shelling in the distance had by now ceased. The fighting had moved on from our vicinity. News of the war was delivered by official notices put up by Tang's soldiers. Travel was still restricted. In fact, there were no more deliveries of certain goods to the village. Whatever supply lines left were now cut off because of the fighting. The village became wholly self-sufficient; we had always fished and grown vegetables, but tools, hardware, and rice used to be shipped in. The shortage of rice in particular was felt.

Mister Wu suffered even more now. He said he would soon run out of goods to sell, and what then?

'How is Li now?'

This was the question Johnny asked me unexpectedly one day.

'Is she keeping well?'

'Yes, she's fine,' I answered.

'Good,' he said. 'Delighted to hear it.'

I couldn't tell whether he meant it or not. Could Johnny be sarcastic? I had noticed how much he had changed from the Johnny I used to know. He was no longer the lively Johnny, full of stories and fun. The older people in the queue used to remark among themselves that it was such responsibility he now carried: being on the village committee, dispensing the village's fish quotas, and looking after old Uncle Zhang – 'Couldn't be easy,' they whispered in agreement.

Johnny didn't ever call round anymore to see Li or myself and I had stopped asking Li whether she missed him a long time back. She refused to answer. I just guessed they had gotten tired of each other, so it was a surprise when he asked about her.

Then Lao, who was busy stacking fish into a barrel beside Johnny, spoke:

'Li? She is looking well, anyway. I saw her two days ago, and looks healthy to me. She has gained weight, I'd say.'

Johnny blushed. He had been letting me have the biggest fish in the quota to bring home. Lao then made a gesture with his hand, covering his tummy while hanging his tongue out. Johnny caught this and I saw his eyes widening. He elbowed Lao to shut up.

I was unsure if Johnny was fooling around or serious, or if a fight would break out.

'Back to work, comrades, the people need to be fed' – It was old Zhang walking towards us with one arm in a sling.

'To each according to his needs, as Marx dictated', 'and Lao Tzu says *Be content with what you have, rejoice in the way things are. When you realize there is nothing lacking, the whole world belongs to you,* 'he laughed and spat.

Zhang was sober today, unusually. He did not even smell like an old bottle today.

'Uncle Zhang,' said Johnny. 'I wasn't expecting you.'

Lao nodded respectfully at Zhang.

'I am here to celebrate,' said Zhang.

'How so?' said Johnny.

To this, old Zhang lifted off his cap and cheered. 'Shanghai – that old whore Shanghai – has fallen!'

He let out a whoop.

'What?' said Lao. 'No?'

Johnny just looked down at his feet, staying quiet; he seemed to be uneasy.

I could hear cheering from up in the village street. People seemed delighted; the news must have just come through. The evening was balmy and calm. It was so different from the fall of Nanking a few weeks ago when everybody then feared the Communists. Why, now we are *all* Communists I suppose!

It was then I thought of the jolly revellers who danced and drank and smoked in all their finery, men and women, in that nightclub the night we found Johnny. It was as if they were celebrating the imminent collapse of their world order. What had become of them? I asked myself – then I thought of Gingko – how had he fared? It was this thought that made me want to go visit Père O.

Along the way to Père O's, villagers were exchanging hugs and handshakes, joyful over the news of Shanghai. Why and how had they changed so much since finding out about Nanking only a few weeks earlier?

And what, I wondered, did old Zhang-ze mean by 'that old whore Shanghai'? Was this another Lao Tzu remark of his?

Approaching Père O's hut, the two guards were smiling dreamily. I soon discovered why – they were sharing a bottle of rice wine, passing it between each other for slugging, backslapping each other every time. I could go inside without bother.

Père O opened the door wearing spectacles. On my way in, one of the guards leaned down to offer me the bottle to drink. I shook my head politely and the soldier swore something, then turned to his comrade, ignoring me while I entered.

Inside, Père O asked me what all the commotion was about.

'It's Shanghai. It has fallen,' I said, imagining everything I saw in the city falling down.

'Fallen to Mao's Red Army?' he said. 'Now this will be interesting.' But he said no more about what he meant. Adults come out with some intriguing comments that I could not quite grasp their meaning. I must work harder on understanding, I decided then.

'I'm afraid I've mislaid the catechism we're studying,' said Père O without even searching first for it. 'You'll have to come back tomorrow instead.'

When I went outside, the guards were drunk and laughing. They were laughing at Chen and Lee, who were throwing stones at Misha, who growled at them. Misha didn't like fat Chen, I could tell.

'Leave her alone,' I shouted.

'That dog is my supper someday,' Chen shouted back pointing to his large stomach. Lee's head went back in laughter, his hands buried deep in his pockets. I half expected the two soldiers to back me up, but they were too pissed drunk.

'Are you not fed up with listening to that priest?' Lao asked me one day.

'No. Why?'

'What does he talk about to you?'

'He tells me his religion.'

'And do you want to learn all about that?'

'It *is* kind of interesting.'

'All about the Christian God who died on a cross?'

'Well, yes, although we haven't gotten that far into it yet.'

Lao shrugged and took out a cigarette. 'No shortage of these yet, anyway.' He grinned, tapping the fresh cigarette against the packet. They were, I noticed, *Lucky Strikes*. Johnny, who had been listening to this while tying nets, said with a broad smile: 'Lao Tzu is the only philosophy.'

'According to Zhang. Anyhow,' Lao laughed.

'There is no religion now,' said Johnny then, assuming a serious face.

'The Council has decreed this.' The Committee that ran the village had changed its name to the Council now.

'Tang doesn't like religion?' said Lao.

'Only the one religion for Comrade Tang,' said Johnny. '...and that's Karl Marx.'

'Mao Tse-tung will approve,' said Lao. 'What made our Tang a communist?'

'Beats me,' said Johnny.

'You best quit visiting the priest,' Lao went on. 'It will be unpopular.'

I said nothing. I looked at Johnny for reassurance. He nodded at me through piercing eyes.

'Really?' I said then.

Then Lao said: 'And best tell your sister that, too.'

'What's that?' said Johnny, surprised. Lao took his cigarette out and blew smoke in rings. They were both working on nets.

'Li...I've seen her leaving the priest's house many times – in the evening,' said Lao.

'You have?' said Johnny, curious. 'Did you know this?' He asked me.

'Um, no,' I said. In truth I did not know. I knew she *used* to visit because I spotted his books lying about the house, but I didn't know she still did.

'Tell her it is against the law now,' said Johnny, pulling even harder on the net he was stitching, his cheeks reddening and puffed out. Lao just glanced over at me and lifted his eyes heavenwards, still smoking his cigarette.

Then one evening I went out the back yard to feed Misha. Li wasn't home, she was out. I had gathered some small pieces of sweetcorn and potato skins for Misha. Rice was now scarce; no more supplies came to the village. Mister Wu was clearly upset but his store remained open.

When I went round the back there was no sign of Misha. Her rope and all was gone. I searched the woodshed and yard calling her. Then I ran back to the front street. Where was Li when I needed her?

On the street I called out for Misha. It was evening, mild and balmy. Some village dogs ran away from me when I called her, as if frightened by me or by something else. I couldn't think of where to go searching. My Misha! What has happened? So, I thought to go to Père O's house for help. I ran towards the shack where he set up his church. His hut was round the back. Passing by the stream I heard sounds coming from the hedges on the hilltop beyond the stream – voices. Something came to mind. Something that forced me to go and investigate.

I walked up the grassy slope with much apprehension, thinking maybe I should go back, that this wasn't my business. Then I heard whispers…and an animal whining. I crept along the slope to find a gap in the bushes. I found a space. Bending down to spy inside I recognised the sounds, their voices, Chen and Lee. There they were sitting inside the gap on big stone rocks. Chen held Misha by her rope. Misha's tail was low between her legs and she was whining low sounds. She cowered before him. Chen and Lee scratched their heads as if planning something. It looked like they had just got here before me.

'What now?' said Lee. 'Now we have her.'

'She is dogfood,' said Chen with determination.

'How? How do we kill her to eat?'

Chen scratched his chin.

'This,' he said, pulling out a knife. Misha cowered even lower at Chen's feet and begged at him with her front paw. I was scared, I admit, but I felt such compassion for Misha.

Lee then said: 'Are you really going to kill the dog, Chen? I just thought we would steal it.'

'I want to taste it,' said Chen. 'I want to taste dog,' he said, feeling Misha's rear leg with his fat, chunky hand.

'But you don't know how to kill it,' said Lee. 'Let's leave the mangy dog.'

'Dogs are a delicacy,' said Chen.

I felt a surge of panic hit me. I really wished I was grown up so I could charge in, beat them up, and rescue Misha. In truth I had no idea what I could do. So I called out to Misha. Misha heard my call and whined out loud. I saw Chen grab her throat.

'Quiet, dog! Or I kill you!'

Lee came out and grabbed me. I screamed loudly. I was thrown to the ground and it hurt.

'Shut him up,' I heard Chen roar at Lee. I was being kicked so I held my hands around my head for protection, screaming all the while. Then I heard scuffling and voices. Voices I could recognise.

'Get off the kid.'

'You bastard!'

Then more scuffles, then Misha yelping. She is dead, I thought. I felt my hand being tugged and I was pulled to my feet. I opened my eyes. It was Lao and Johnny. I looked and saw both Chen and Lee running down the slope towards the village. Johnny held Misha by the length of rope and handed it over to me.

'You ought to be more careful of your dog.'

'What could he do, Johnny? They were way bigger than him.'

Poor Misha licked me all over and I rubbed her furry body hard.

'Good dog, Misha, good dog. You're safe now.'

I looked at Johnny. 'Thank you, Johnny.'

Johnny nodded and said, 'Not me. It was Lao here recognised your voice and said we must help.'

'Thank you, Lao.' I bowed. Lao blushed, saying, 'That's alright, kid,' punching my shoulder.

We walked back down to the village together. Just before we parted our separate ways, Lao pointed towards Père O's house. When we looked over we saw Père O embracing Li, then without either of them speaking, Li walked away towards home. They did not see us.

'Why are you not married, Li?'

This I casually asked one night as Li was busy washing her dark hair over a basin. I felt she looked so pretty. She stood upright to rinse it back.

'Why do you ask?' she said without any irritation in her voice. I was only too surprised she was not so surprised by my question.

'All the girls your age are either married or with boyfriends,' I said, pretending to be more concerned with looking into the fire than with her.

'I have no-one to court me,' she said out of the blue. I was holding a long stick into the flame and thought about this.

'But there was Johnny...' I said eventually, and prepared for the worst.

'Don't be daft,' she said, continuing her rinse.

'No?'

'No.'

'And there's no-one else?'

She looked around with her big eyes – this I was prepared for.

'How do you mean? She said.

I hesitated a bit, then.

'You don't like any others?'

She held her hands on her hips, then spoke.

'Do you realise there is a war? That a lot of boys from the village have gone to fight? And before this, before we fought each other, there were the Japanese to fight?'

I stayed silent, thinking as she found a towel to dry her hair.

'Tang is back now,' I suddenly blurted out. She slowly stopped drying her hair, her motions slowed now, turned away from me, and I could swear she was sobbing gently.

'I wish they all stayed away,' she said. 'Men.'

The Conversation

Fr Kiely was now inspecting the bookshelves as if searching for some volume, the lined hardbacks on parade so to speak. He found the one.

'This is more your line.' He plonked the book on the table in front of Père Olivier. The Father read the cover – 'The Letters and Instructions of St Francis Xavier'.

'Right-hand man to St Ignatius,' said Père Olivier.

'A missionary,' Fr Kiely said.

'He travelled much,' agreed Père Olivier.

'Yes, a traveller and a missionary. You can be both.'

'Depends on the journey.'

'All journeys to God are unique to the traveller. And consequently personal.'

Is he really one of us? Fr Kiely wondered. I mean fourteen years to ordination as a 'J'. Surely anything 'odd' would have been sussed.

'What's the fascination with Milton and the "lost Eden"?' Fr Kiely asked, leaning over Olivier's shoulder and fingering the

marked line in the open book spread on the table, like a primary teacher checking on a pupil.

Père Olivier gave him a glance, then answered:

'Just that..."lost Eden", and how.'

'How?'

'The woman was tempted.'

'Before the man was?'

'Precisely.'

'Women are weak?'

Père Olivier appeared to blush. Some emotions cannot be hidden.

'They are strong, they bring life into the world, this nurture is felt, too,' said Père Olivier.

'But they need care, attention, for they have weakness – for temptation. Much more than men, they are more easily seduced.

'Nevertheless, remember the man in the Garden neglected his duty also. He should have protected his woman,' Fr Kiely checked himself.

'Expelled from Paradise?' Fr Kiely made another move.

Père Olivier nodded.

'Forbidden fruit,' said Kiely.

A girl twenty years his junior! Well, could be worse – and how it'd have come back on us…the company, had it been the opposite – Caesar's weakness. Fr Kiely groaned inwardly thinking this. All types, he thought. Still he didn't do anything. No, just became infatuated. His student and all. Pity.

'Of course, it's only allegorical, the Genesis story,' explained Père Olivier.

'Are you a disciple of our brother… the reverend Teilhard de Chardin SJ?'

'I've certainly read him, Father.'

'He fully accepts Darwin and that we're all evolving to some Omega point. The whole bloody universe,' Fr Kiely reasoned. All types indeed.

'Then there is the opinion that everything recurs. That it's all cyclical…human history,' Père Olivier went on.

'That history moves from the age of gods and heroes to an aristocratic phase to democratic to chaos and back again.'

'Interesting,' said Fr Kiely.

'Very,' said Père Olivier. 'The Irish writer James Joyce, it's said, constructs this in his last work, Finnegans Wake.*'*

'Gibberish.'

Père Olivier lifted an eyebrow to query this. Dan Kiely caught it.

'He also writes in it about a Fall and includes The Fall of Man, of Lucifer, of other characters fictional and historical.'

'Finnegans Wake,' said Kiely, 'Totally incomprehensible, I'm told, by those who know. Who knew Joyce.'

'One of our own,' said Père Olivier.

'The Reverend James Joyce, SJ?' Fr Kiely joked. ' Hmm... Our lost progeny. A former prefect of sodality. Yes, we failed there alright.'

'All a beautiful lie,' said Père Olivier with a smirk.

'Pardon? Jacques.'

'What Joyce is alleged to have said about his faith...in the end, of course,' Père Olivier explained.

Have we failed again? Fr Kiely wondered, glancing sidelong at Père Olivier.

Fr Kiely gripped his fist in his palm. Might as well cut to the chase.

'You like the military feel of Ignatius?'

Père Olivier looked at the Dean.

'I'm more an Xavier man.' He smiled his yellowing teeth.

Fr Kiely inclined his head towards the book he had just laid before Olivier.

'The missionary in me,' said Père Olivier.

For a whole day the sky became grey all of a sudden. A sticky humid atmosphere invaded the air and suddenly, that night, the warm, balmy evenings we had been having gave way to a downpour. A deluge. The thunder cracked the skies open and the clouds emptied as if their underbellies had been slit emptying their contents earthwards. It cleared the street, sending people running home and scattering the dust and dirt to rivulets of brown, muddy water, running along its length. Nature's elements work independently of each other; the winds and rain do not cease for darkness yet the sun does. Neither does heat stop when the sun, its source, sets.

Misha did not like to hear thunder. I had often heard old Zhang say 'you must listen to thunder', always in company when somebody would say something he did not like or agree with. Misha howled her woeful sound out the back of the house. I had tied her in the woodshed. The rain bucketed on the roof, rattling the tin. It came down so heavy and the thunder roared so hard me and Li both looked at each other in shock. Then Li burst out laughing, saying, 'Old Zhang-ze will not be dry tonight.'

'Nobody will,' I said.

Li went to boil water to make tea while I stared out the window at the deluge. Why, even now I remember that night whenever rainstorms come. I love staring at the rain from the shelter and warmth of somewhere safe. I always felt a feeling of safety being under a roof while it downpoured outside – a sense of being secure, and dry, and warm. The street was cleared of people, the rain formed pools in the mud. Misha howled and howled.

'I must see to her,' I said to Li.

'What? Are you mad?'

'She is frightened,' I said.

'It is a dog,' she snapped.

'She is mine,' I answered.

'And you are mine,' she said.

But I could not bear hearing her howls, so when Li wasn't looking for once, I unlatched the door and ran round the back to the woodshed. I only wanted to comfort Misha.

I got drenched just running from the front of the house to the back, my clothes, hair, face, all wet. I pulled open the door saying, 'Here, Misha, it's alright, girl'. But as soon as it opened, she bolted out, making a getaway.

She ran terrified, in no particular direction, just straight ahead. I roared, 'Misha, come back!'

I followed her direction, soaked to the skin. Half-blinded by the torrential downpour, I followed on, calling her.

I feared she would run to the forest where I would never find her; or run into the path of Chen and Lee. I feared this would happen. The noise of thunder and the rattling rain filled my ears. I went along the street in the direction of the River. I approached Père O's old church – the Parish Church of Zhaoui, Père O's residence at the rear. There appeared to be no guards to get drenched on duty tonight.

Then whining, whimpering, or low yelp-like sounds. I turned to go right. I heard it more clearly now: a dog. I went closer to the church building, and there I saw Misha, crouching down in the doorway.

'Misha, girl,' I called to her. But she just crouched even lower, lifting her hind leg in submission, no visible tail moving.

I approached her slowly so as not to scare her. I had almost reached her and I think she recognised me for she began to crawl forward in my direction. Then suddenly from the skies it struck, like an arrow from the heavens: a lightning bolt. It flashed all around me in a dazzle of light; the sound came later when I was stretched on the mud-wet ground. I felt I was paralysed. Then someone slapping my cheeks. I opened my eyes. Li was looking into them speaking, but I could not hear. She firmly slapped me again on the ears till I heard ringing and came to. The first thing I said was:

'Where is Misha?'

Li gestured for me to look behind. I looked and saw Johnny holding Misha by her half-chewed rope.

'You are lucky,' Li said, vexed. 'You were almost killed. Do you not know to stay away from under trees and from dogs in lightning storms?'

I simply looked at her, dazed.

'It is a good job Père O has put a lightning deflector on the roof of his little church,' she said.

I didn't understand what she was talking about.

'He says all churches have them where he comes from – to protect community, he says.'

'How do you know this?' said Johnny suddenly. 'He has told you?'

The rain still poured down.

'Let's go,' said Johnny then. 'I'm getting soaked.'

On our way home, Li spoke to me: 'I noticed you gone, and I ran out to find you. Then I saw both you and the dog were gone. So I went to the church, and on the way I passed Johnny bringing his uncle home from cards.'

Johnny made a yawn as if he didn't care or was pretending not to listen.

'He lost again,' he put in eventually.

Suddenly, Li jerked up and we all stopped. What now? I wondered. She felt her tummy again with her hand, while rubbing her other hand through her wet hair, like she did when thinking deeply.

'It's nothing,' she said. 'Let's go.'

We reached the house and I put Misha back in the woodshed, this time tying an even better knot to her piece of rope. When I went inside Johnny and Li were arguing.

'What is this? Are you carrying?' he gestured with his hands, while gaping at her stomach.

'Johnny,' she pleaded.

'Answer me.'

'Johnny.' She turned away, her hand on her cheek.

'Yes, you are!' he shouted.

'Who was it with?' Johnny demanded.

'Please, Johnny...'

'I know who – so tell me...'

Li's face looked frozen and she did not answer. I never before saw my sister Li stuck for any words, she was always so smart. Johnny poised to raise his hand to her.

'Leave!' I shouted at him. 'Leave my sister alone!'

'You...' Johnny blurted at Li, 'You...'

Then he hurried out the door, and I imagined I saw tears in his face, but it could have been the rain. Li bit her fist and trembled. I rushed to embrace her.

'What is it, Li?'

I had little sleep so rose early. I brought Li some breakfast to her bed – some fruit only. It was becoming clear to me now that there were some shortages of food, something to do with the war, and late-stage capitalism, Tang added in a notice he posted in the general store.

Li sat up wearily rubbing her eyes and said to leave it beside the bed. I knew she would not eat but I did as she said. I had already checked on Misha who was fast asleep this morning. It was still early but I would call on Zhu later and we would go walking, then I decided I would go to Père O to learn more about God. But I would be careful because of what Lao told me. I wanted to ask Père O what to do about Chen and Lee, who seemed to have a dislike of Misha and me.

I looked out the window – the morning was bright. The thunder of the night before had cleared all the grey clouds and heavy sticky atmosphere away, and the day looked promising. Already the sun had appeared over the hills to our east in a red semi-circle. Bird-life was starting the day with chirping sounds.

I would be good to Li today, I thought. So I started to clean the house. I swept floors. I cleaned pots. I counted the foodstuffs we had; only a half sack of rice and some peppers remained.

The morning passed slowly. People appeared on the street, going about their chores as usual. I was tidying up something when I heard thuds outside the door, the clunk of footsteps...thump...thump...two knocks...loud. I hesitated. Who could this be?

Before, I could tell Li was nervous of any association with Tang being discovered and the authorities calling round. But now the Red Army controlled the region and it was Tang in charge.

I thought then of Chen and Lee. Perhaps they were pulling a trick on me? But would even they be bold enough to call early in the morning? I thought yes...

I waited for them to go away. I listened closely at the door. I heard whispering voices. It must be them. I did not move or even breathe. I thought then they could hear my heart beating, so loud was it. Then I thought of Misha. Was Misha safe?

'Open up. We know you're there,' a loud voice demanded. This wasn't Chen.

'Who is there?' I said to the shut door.

'We have orders to arrest Li-tan, who lives here.'

'It is the People's' Army,' another voice said.

'Why? What is wrong?' I asked. Then I felt something on my shoulder. It was Li. She had come up behind me. She motioned me to step aside. I did, slowly, and she opened the latch.

A Red Army soldier bearing a slip of paper along with two other soldiers pointing rifles were standing outside. The soldier with the paper looked nervous. He studied Li's face; his own face seemed embarrassed. Then he coughed awkwardly and said:

'Li-tan?'

Li nodded without speaking. The soldier then nodded and looked down at the paper and read aloud:

'Li-tan, I am ordered to detain you on the charge of collaborating with the enemy, and of the charge of receiving illegal instructions in a forbidden activity.'

'What?' Li said, feeling her tummy. I surely thought she would collapse.

'Please come with us, Li-tan,' the soldier said sternly.

Li stared into the soldier's nervous blue eyes.

'Who has made this order? she asked.

'My orders are signed by Commander Tang-lee,' the soldier said.

'And who is accusing me?' she then demanded.

'Please come.' The soldier held his arm out.

'Where are you taking her?' I said, standing between Li and the soldiers. One of them then pushed me aside and went to take Li, but she lifted her hand and spoke quietly.

'No. Leave me. I will go so.'

'Li,' I said, 'Don't.'

Li bent down to face me, her hands on my shoulders.

'I must,' she said. 'You must be brave,' she told me.

Then, wiping a tear, she stood again. She walked off following the little soldier in charge, followed by the other two guards carrying their rifles.

People gazed on in amazement. I realised this would be the subject of much gossip in the village. I knew I must tell Père O. So, when they were out of sight, I locked the door behind me and went to Père O's house. It was getting hotter now; it would be a good day – weather-wise. Whatever heavy humidity had been in the atmosphere had been cleared by the rain and thunder last night.

Coming towards Père O's, I saw there were no guards on the door. Have they left him alone now? Was he now a free man?'

I walked up to the front door. There was a sign posted, written in red:

FORBIDDEN TO ENTER
BY ORDER
Tang-lee,
District Commander, Zhaoui

Disbelieving what I read, I banged my fist hard on the door.

'I wouldn't do that if I were you,' said a voice.

'He has been brought away for questioning,' said another.

'For good,' laughed another.

'Yeah, you best clear off, kid.'

'Yes, your friend the priest has been arrested. You might too, if you hang around here.'

Two elderly villagers who were approaching said this. Père O was arrested? How was this?

'Why did they take him?' I asked.

One of the old boys grinned at me.

'Because his religion has been banned, I guess,' and the other laughed.

I went to walk away, and as I was leaving, the two were peeping through the keyhole and the window.

'What do you see?' one said.

'Nothing. Anything of value they took away with them.'

'Yes, I saw all the silver platters and cups being carted off.'

'No more religion, then.'

'Only old books in there now.'

I left them to their scrutinising and scavenging of Père O's residence and went towards home. I passed villagers doing their routine daily tasks. How could they, I thought, when Li and Père O were taken off just like that? Everyone appeared oblivious to this and to me, and yet, as they walked by I felt they all knew and didn't trust me anymore. Nobody spoke to me. I walked home, and the first thing I did was check in on Misha in the back woodshed. When I looked in she was cowering in the dark, but as soon as I called her, she leaped up to lick my hands and face, tail going in circles.

I didn't go back in the house then. I just sat there in the dark for most of the day, rocking back and forth with Misha in my arms, thinking, what now? In truth I was confused. The night came and passed. Cicadas chipped and toad noises from the stream filled the silence in the darkness outside – a warm and humid night. I slept lightly and woke a few times, having had many dreams. In each dream life was happy and normal – Li was there, and in another, so were father and mother. Yet each time I woke up, the dream dissolved, dissipating into the thin night air, and the reality of my present situation came back. Which was the dream and which the reality? I wondered. They seemed so real and so immediate, these 'dreams'.

What, I thought, if this 'reality' was all a dream and I would awake suddenly and Li would be here again? Or even father and mother? What if my whole life so far, and Zhu, Johnny, Zhang, Père O, had all been a dream, as before I had funny dreams and I would awake to a different reality? As the grey dawn crept under the shut door I felt so tired, like I hadn't slept a wink. I remained there holding onto Misha as morning came. I had nowhere to go anyway. I was suddenly scared. What if the soldiers took me away next? I did not stir.

Some hours passed and I heard noise. I sat up alert...and listened. Footsteps I was sure. First, on the boardwalk in front of the house, then a rat-a-tat-tat knocking. The soldiers have come back,

I knew it. This time for me! I lay very quiet. Good job I was out here. Misha began sniffing at the door. Then the noises ceased. I felt relief. Then Misha was on her feet again, smelling the air in the gap at the bottom of the door.

'Be quiet, girl,' I whispered, grabbing her tail. I listened closely. There was someone moving round the back of the house. They are on to me, I thought then. So I lay crouched behind the few logs of wood in the pile trying to grip Misha's fur to quieten her. If they hear her we are truly gone. There was movement outside. The latch on the door was rattling. It suddenly opened and light entered. Misha stood wagging her tail. Oh no, I am caught, I knew it. But still I lay low behind the wood. Somebody entered, I saw a shadow. I opened my eyes and a face peered from above down at me:

'Zhu!'

Misha was all over him with licking and tail wagging non-stop.

'Why are you here?' Zhu said.

I felt embarrassed then and tried to tell him what had happened to Li.

'But I know,' said Zhu. 'Mother told me...everyone knows.'

'And the priest, too,' he added.

I stared at him.

'I wanted to check if you were still here. Are you alright?'

'I…I think so,' I said, clutching Misha.

'Have you enough food? You know this war means things are getting scarce, Mother says.'

'I think so, too,' I said, remembering the half sack of rice and the few peppers we had. I was thinking Johnny could get me enough fish and I could qualify for vegetables.

Zhu then looked about him.

'Phew,' he said. 'What are you doing out here – in this place?'

Not wanting to let on I was scared, I quickly came out with:

'It's a game.'

Zhu's eyes shone at this, he laughed. 'What game? Tell me.'

'I am hiding from the soldiers…and so is Misha – it's pretend.'

Zhu thought about this a bit, then he laughed some more.

'That is a good game.'

I nodded in assent, both glad and relieved he swallowed it. Zhu was in many ways like his mother.

'Can I play, too?' He said then.

'Oh, yes.' I thought fast.

'You can bring round some food. But don't tell anyone about me being out here, or about our game.'

'This is a funny game,' said Zhu.

Misha, sensing Zhu's excitement, stood and pawed at him. Zhu laughed, showing his familiar gap-toothed smile, and tried to brush Misha's attention off.

It was settled then. Zhu would bring food. I would ask Johnny for fish even though I wasn't yet able to cook. I would hide here in the woodshed should the soldiers or anybody else come to the house looking for me. I had it all worked out.

One evening after calling round Zhu was preparing to leave when he blurted out:

'You know there's going to be a trial?'

I looked at him, puzzled.

'A what?'

'The trial,' he said. 'Li and old Xi, and the priest are to be tried by court,' Zhu said, acting with authority, like one who knew what he was talking about...I didn't.

'What is this?'

'I don't know. Mother said,' he said then, bashful, afraid of my reaction.

'She read it on some notice – in the village.'

We had never heard of such things in Zhaoui before – a trial?

'Where will this be? When?' I said.

'In five days, I think,' said Zhu, teasing Misha with some food morsels.

As soon as Zhu had left I decided to find out more for myself. I went out of the woodshed. I had expected to encounter hostility from the villagers because of Li, and my relationship with Père O. But to my surprise nobody even noticed me or bothered with me. People simply carried on as normal as both me and Misha wandered around. I found we could walk about unnoticed as before. One or two even nodded friendly at me and one old man laughed at Misha. I began to feel safe outside again. Perhaps, I thought, this will all pass and Li will return home again. Even passing some soldiers, they paid me no attention. So I went over to Wu's General Store. There, as usual, were old people drinking tea outside, three men. Old Wu must be inside.

I walked up the wooden steps. On the public notice board I spotted it – the official notice from Tang nailed up. I read it:

Chinese Communist Party

NOTICE TO THE PEOPLE OF ZHAOUI

THE TRIAL OF THE FOLLOWING FOR VARIOUS OFFENCES WILL BE HELD IN PUBLIC ON

Friday, June 20, 1949

Xi-lo,
Li-tan,
Jacques Olivier, Laowai.

By Order,
Tang-lee,
District Commander, Zhaoui.

So Zhu's nosey mother had got it right. Five days' time it would be. Li and Père O would be tried. And Mister Xi, too? Why him?

The old men sitting drinking tea were smoking cigarettes and talking.

'What will happen to them?'

The sour-faced one gestured the cut-throat with his finger. The others looked at him.

'Naw,' one said. 'They will get off. What have they done exactly?'

'They broke the law.'

'Tang's law...and the girl and Tang?' the other said. I listened closely when he said this, curious to learn more.

'What about old Xi?'

'He's a goner, definitely,' said the sour-faced one, and they all coughed laughter.

'Poor Xi.'

Then, as if he were listening in, Mister Wu came out holding a brush and everyone shut up. He glanced around, then looked me and Misha up and down.

'You want to feed that dog,' he said. 'Fatten it up,' he said, grinning at the three men.

This is a strategy I notice in people to win favour with others or to change the attention; they will pick on the soft target. I do not know if I or Misha was his intended butt, but as he said this he swept the dirt off the sideboard onto Misha. The three looked at me and Misha.

'Oh, it's that kid again.'

'With his supper,' said one with a fish-like mouth, and then laughed showing fish teeth to match.

'*Our* supper,' another said.

'Don't be giving me ideas,' said Wu, basking in his success. It then occurred to me that I had noticed the dog population in the village getting smaller.

'More tea, Wu,' the sour-faced man said.

'What do you think I am?' Wu glared. 'Tea is scarce now, like everything.'

'No tea in China?' the man said.

'As a matter of fact, yes, deliveries are few and far between.'

'First rice, now tea. China is ruined,' said the man again.

Mister Wu ceased sweeping then and looked up and down the street. He gestured the button-your-lip signal with his finger and the men all nodded understanding. They continued on then exhaling smoke quietly till they looked like they were surrounded by a blue haze.

It was Tang himself who appeared on the street in front of the store.

'Well, Wu?' he said, ascending the wooden steps.

'How is business today?'

'Business, you call it? Giving away everything.'

Tang did not address me but he lay his hand on my head as he stood there at my side surveying the scene. The old men remained silent but nodded at him, still puffing away, observing.

'To each to his needs. Don't you feel better contributing to the village? Working for all instead of for your own profit?' Tang said, winking at the three men.

'I am not happy giving my hard-earned goods away free,' Wu said in a huff.

'But you did not produce the goods, any goods. Some poor worker far away did it. He should be rewarded, not you who sell them at a profit.'

'That is business,' said Wu. 'That's my business.'

'Exactly,' said Tang. 'I could give you literature to explain our position – the party's position,' he went on. 'People must be educated...and others,' he said staring directly at Wu. 'Re-educated.'

Wu met Tang's eyes, and lowered his, then he made a deliberate sweep with his brush scattering dirt onto Misha. Tang did not like this. He lay his hand tight on my shoulder. He said, 'Ah, nature's hierarchy. Man over beast.' Then, to Wu: 'Be careful your hierarchy order doesn't transfer to your fellow man.'

'It's already happened,' blurted the sour-faced man, ending the silence of the three.

'And that,' Tang said, 'is what we're here to end.'

He stepped forward and took out his pack of cigarettes, offering one to each of the old men. After lighting theirs and taking one himself, he turned to all and said:

'"We come to abolish the village idiot," said Lenin. A noble ideal. No-one is above anyone else…that's our policy.'

I wanted to speak up and say that Misha was my family and equal, but I was afraid to. Tang made me nervous and I was afraid they might laugh at me for being stupid. Wu looked uneasy, sweeping the brush with long, fast sweeps.

'Hmm,' he said. 'Easy to distribute nothing.'

'Pardon?' said Tang.

'When I have no goods left, everyone gets nothing. Is that just?'

'That people get nothing is neither just nor acceptable. Would you like it if only two could afford to buy?'

'Well, yes,' said Wu.

'So two benefit while the rest starve? Is that just?'

'It mightn't be fair, but it's called commerce.'

'Commerce?' nodded Tang in slow movements. Then he dragged on his cigarette and slowly blew rings of smoke.

'You see,' he appealed to the men. 'We need to completely transform from capitalist society and completely re-educate the ignorant.'

'You are the village idiot, Wu', the fish-toothed man laughed. The other two grinned but said nothing. Mister Wu used to provide them with tea daily. I knew, even then, that they knew when to behave themselves.

'Is there re-education for my cousin Xi, then?' Wu said in a low voice. Tang, hearing this, spun around. 'That is for the court to decide.'

'And the *Laowai* priest? ...And the girl?' Wu then said.

'Also for the court to decide,' said Tang. Mister Wu stopped his sweeping and stood holding the broom. Tang took a final drag on his cigarette then tossed it on the ground and quenched it with his boot. He bowed in respect. 'I must go now. Good day, gentlemen.' The three nodded, still silent. Tang walked down the steps then swiftly turned round.

'By the way, Wu, there is a shipment of fruit arriving tomorrow. Make sure to keep some oranges for my men.'

Wu stood still leaning on the broom. He just grunted. Then Tang looked at me, pointed a finger, and curled it.

'Come with me, lad,' he gestured.

What was this? Was I now being arrested as well? What did I do? Tang snapped his fingers.

'Come, come,' he said lightly and walked away with his long strides. I followed slowly, yet unsure what would happen. He may be bringing me to see Li, or to tell me he will release her. That it was all a mistake. To let me take her home again maybe.

He marched all the way to the Red Army encampment just outside the land entrance to the village, me following. The tents were large and wide, lined up in two rows facing each other. We walked along the path between them. At the end of the row he suddenly turned and disappeared into the mouth of a wide canvas tent.

I walked along after him, past the lines of tents, hearing voices coming out of some of them in different dialects, smells of garlic and cooking wafted about. I came to his tent. Outside I hesitated, afraid to enter. I thought about going back. Then he called.

'Come in. Have some fruit.'

I peeked inside. It looked dark and smelled different than the outside; a grassy odour, and leather or canvas. Without thinking I suddenly found myself inside, facing him – Tang.

I had known him since I was little and he called round to see Li, but he disappeared from the village when I was very young and was only afterwards spoken about in hushed voices. Li never allowed me to speak of him. I did not understand why but it made me frightened of him. He was my bogeyman. Looking back, I think now my fear of the hills and those who dwelt there was really my fear of Tang. Now I was alone with him. He poured himself a cup of tea and offered me one. I shook my head. He smiled and walked towards a dish containing fruit. He plucked an orange from the dish and held it before me, lifting an eyebrow to ask without speaking if I wanted it. It looked tempting, my eyes took in its shape, my mouth watered imagining its sweet flesh and juice. But I shook my head again. Tang could only smile. No words were yet spoken. Then he tossed the fruit at my chest and my knee-jerk reaction was to catch it with both hands. This broke the ice.

'You want it after all.'

I felt myself blushing then, shamed that I had been caught out.

'Please,' I said. 'Let Li go.'

'Hah!' Tang seemed happy. 'You *can* speak.'

He lit a cigarette. I stared at the ground, not answering. He walked around me smoking and studying me like I was a curiosity.

'You are Li's young brother.'

Not knowing if this was a question or not, I looked up.

'Please let her go.' Then down again.

'I would love to,' he said in his sudden manner of speaking. 'I would love to,' he said again, this time more slowly holding his cigarette to his chest.

'But someone has made a complaint – I mean an allegation, against her.'

I looked up, there may have been tears in my eyes, for he said again:

'I have a duty to perform, so I will ask you some questions.'

I was so nervous I could not reply.

'The *Laowai* priest,' he went on. 'How much does she see him, Li?'

I squeezed my eyes shut.

'How many times a day? ...Or night?' he added.

There was a silence.

I felt I was trembling. He must have sensed something, for he said:

'It's alright. I mean you no harm...or Li, either. You know I am very fond of her, your sister.'

I opened my eyes. He stood holding his cigarette with its fumes rising upwards, his eyes looking straight in front in a distant gaze.

'If you only knew,' he said quietly. 'So tell me,' he continued out loud again.

'How many times does she see the priest? How many times has she seen him?'

'I don't know,' I said then.

'Aha,' he said. 'So you *have* a tongue.' He quenched the cigarette in an ashtray on a table. I noticed the inside of the tent now for the first time. A lamp was suspended from a fastener in one of the tent's poles. There was a table scattered with papers, on top of which was the heavy ashtray filled with cigarette ends, two small foldable seats, and behind all this at the rear was a single bunk bed.

'I'm afraid if you cannot tell me I will have to ask somebody who can.' Tang sat on the stool nearest his desk, crossing his legs. Another cigarette was lit up.

'We wait,' he said.

He read some papers then in silence. I was scared.

A minute or so later a guard appeared at the entrance to the tent. Tang looked up.

'You have the prisoner?' he said. The guard clicked his heels and bowed his head. Then he left again only to return with another soldier and Père O himself.

'Leave us,' said Tang. The soldiers bowed and left. Père O looked relaxed but confused. He took in the scene before him saying nothing.

'Sit,' Tang said, indicating the small seat. 'Thank you,' said Père O. He sat down. His long legs looking silly folded up in front of him on the little stool. He looked at me surprised at first, then he nodded to me. Tang held out his cigarettes but Père O refused.

'Ah, I forgot,' said Tang, 'You don't use tobacco – only altar wine.' He smiled.

'Well, I can't offer you any of that...have an orange.' He threw an orange from the dish onto Père O's lap. Père O caught it. Before he had time to peel and eat it, Tang began:

'So, Father...have you been giving your Masses to the people of Zhaoui?'

Père O answered directly, 'Not since you forbade it. No, Commander.'

Tang lifted an eyebrow.

'Really?' Then he said no more. There was silence. Tang held his smoking cigarette in one hand resting on the table, while his right hand held a pen poised to write. The smoke covered him somewhat so I couldn't quite make him out.

'I offer one Mass service for myself daily,' Père O said, clearing his throat.

'Really?' said Tang, his pen poised.

'Yes.'

'And is it just for you, or is anybody else in your presence when you say Mass?'

Père O did not answer this.

Tang waited patiently, staring at the priest. Père O studied the orange within his long fingers.

'You see,' Tang broke the silence. 'It doesn't matter to me what religion anybody practises, it's just the Central Committee has ruled against such practices for the moment in the regions we control.'

Père O stared back.

'The war hasn't been won yet.' Tang smiled as an afterthought.

'Most definitely not,' said Père O. 'The gates of Hell shall not prevail,' he said low under his breath.

Tang laughed and said, 'We are not that bad...We are not anti-God. We are anti-capitalist and anti-imperialist. God is irrelevant. What do we speak of as God? God exists only as the driving force of history over these periods of time, creating change according to the dialectic which Marx refined from Hegel to be: thesis, antithesis, then synthesis. This drives history forward, not some exterior 'God' waving his hands. But it is ultimately man who does the work. Without man, history is static, not dynamic. In fact without man there is no history; everything is sterile.'

Père O said, 'I beg to disagree.'

Tang studied the priest holding the orange.

'That is fruit...am I correct in saying that nowhere in your Christian Bible is an apple mentioned as the forbidden fruit Eve tempted Adam with?'

'You are indeed correct,' said Père O.

'What was the fruit?'

'Scripture – Genesis – mentions the fruit of the tree of knowledge.'

'And no name given?' said Tang.

'None.'

'It would seem, then,' said Tang, 'that the orange is more likely a candidate to be such a fruit than an apple.'

Père O gripped the orange like a baseball. 'How so?'

'The orange,' said Tang, 'contains seeds, can tell us a lot about reproduction in primitive life forms, hence knowledge.'

'So do other fruits,' said Père O.

'Aah,' Tang said then. 'Let me quote Milton with whom you are so familiar:

"Of Man's first disobedience and the fruit of that forbidden tree, whose mortal taste brought death and woe into the world"'

'Hardly the life-giving orange,' said Père O.

'You are a Belgian?' said Tang.

'*Oui,*' said Père O.

'*D'accord,*' continued Tang. 'A French-speaking one – a Walloon?'

'Correct.'

'And to your north the Flemish-speaking protestants and then the Dutch, whose House of Orange brought such woes to your people. Forbidden fruit indeed, bringing such death and woe.'

'That is a coincidence. It's the colour rather than the fruit you're talking about there,' Père O said.

Tang threw his pen on the paper in front of him.

'Just a theory I had,' he said. 'So no Christian Mass for others then?' he said firmly.

Again, Père O did not answer.

'You know I will have to take your silence as an affirmation of guilt?' said Tang.

Père O gestured, what can I do? Tang scribbled some more notes down.

'You.' He pointed at me. 'Has your sister Li-tang ever gone to this man's house for instruction in his religion?'

I suddenly felt the burn of staring directed onto me. I froze, looking to my side at the tent's opening flapping there, daylight penetrating through. What could I do?

'I don't know,' I eventually stammered.

'Certain religious books have been seen in your house,' Tang went on.

When he said this I was truly awakened to what had happened. The only people who could have seen the books were myself, Li, Père O, Tang himself...and Johnny!

As Tang spoke, I ceased listening and only considered who had informed on Li – it must be Johnny. But why?

Tang continued: 'Traditional philosophies and religions all seek to find reason behind man's existence. Let me tell you: man, like all other animals, creatures, is the result of natural selection and evolution.

'Early human societies were communal, but as human bonding got complicated, became based on the productive capacities of people. The productive relations between human beings determined their place in society and the class system developed. First slavery, then feudalism, now it is capitalism, where the ownership of the means of production is in the hands of a significant few. All war and inequality is the result of this.'

'So, no Eden, then?' said Père O, who appeared to be charged up by this debate.

'Oh, Eden can be whatever myth you wish,' said Tang.

Père O examined his orange.

'And oranges?' he questioned.

'Ask the Irish,' said Tang.

I did not understand what Tang meant, but Père O nodded in acknowledgement at this.

'Of course I have heard other metaphorical explanations,' Tang said. 'Some Christian missionaries have claimed that the forbidden fruit mentioned was in fact meat.'

Père O's face registered surprise and interest.

'Yes, once man began to kill animals for food, he had tasted forbidden fruit and also lost his innocence.'

Père O's eyes widened and he nodded again. I thought of Chen and Lee and Misha.

'Anyhow, you may both go,' Tang ordered. 'I'll get nothing more from you two.'

He banged the table with his fist, and as if waiting, the two guards came in to escort Père O away. Before being led off, Père O bent down and gripped my shoulders. He smiled at me and handed me the orange.

'Be good,' he said. 'And watch out for Li...and be careful with Misha.'

Then they left.

Tang lit another cigarette and opened his tunic collar. 'Go. I hope for your sake Li is proven innocent.' His voice sounded weak. He turned his back saying again, 'I truly hope she is innocent.'

I left the tent and untied Misha to walk back to the village.

We left the Red Army encampment behind and walked back to the main street. The day had by now slipped into evening but I couldn't go back home yet. My mind kept thinking about the conversation in Tang's tent. I thought of Tang's remarks about the books Li had. Tang had even lent her some himself, she said. Tang was philosophical in speech but could easily be agitated into action. One of those rare types; pensive and active. But he could hardly have sent his own soldiers round on his own evidence, what excuse would he give for his involvement with Li?

Li and Père O never told anyone about them, of that I was sure, nor did I. So Johnny then? Did Johnny tell on Li? I would go to old Zhang's house and, whether he be drunk or not, I would challenge Johnny right there.

On the brown dirt of the broad street I felt something...phshutt...it hit the dirt path in front of us. Then another one. I looked to the sky. It was not rain? Then a sting on my arm...Ouch! I had been hit by something. Then Misha yelped, turning her head to her rump. There were no mosquitoes or gnats about. What was this? I was hit again on my hand – it was a pebble. We were being fired on. Was this now the Kuomintang who were attacking our village?

Then I heard laughter I recognised – Chen and Lee's voices jeering and teasing. I looked up. They were on the porch of the general store firing at Misha and me with a hand-held catapult. The store was closed now in the evening. The street was deserted. People must be having supper.

The stones ricocheted on the dirt on the dirt street. Some stung when they hit their targets. Misha galloped off ahead while I turned to face Chen and Lee, big grins on their faces as they jeered.

'That dog is fat enough for eating.'

'Yeah, when your sister's gone, we come for you.'

Still aiming the slingshot at Misha, I roared at them to stop, to leave us alone. Then, as Chen stood to aim again I ran up close and gripping the orange Père O gave me, I hurled it straight at him...splaat! It landed on his fat cheek exploding all over his face with orange pus. I ran as fast as I could with Misha following me nipping at my heels with excitement.

I ran with the shouts of Chen behind us, letting me know what they will do with me and Misha once Li 'is gone'. And it was this that urged me to go straight to old Zhang's house to confront Johnny. I ran through the neglected garden at the front of their house. I could smell cooking inside. I knocked and Johnny opened.

'It's you again. Come on in, we're about to eat.'

Inside, old Zhang sat in front of a fire where there was a pot suspended cooking food. I smelled rice. Old Zhang did not acknowledge me. He simply stared at the flames while feeling his wounded arm with his good hand. There was the stink of wine about the place though the table was bare of any bottles, with just two bowls set for supper.

Johnny directed me to sit by the fire with Zhang. He removed the pot from hanging above the fire and spooned rice into the bowls. It was steaming and it looked and smelled good.

'Uncle, here is supper,' said Johnny, as he sat down and began filling his mouth with the rice. I had not eaten good rice for days, Zhu told me it was scarce now. I looked at Zhang. He still had the unshaven face of uneven, grey stubble, still wore his cap indoors. He seemed to be in his own world there, speaking to himself and staring at the fire.

'It's good rice, Uncle,' said Johnny. 'Just as you like it.'

'I exchanged our fish quota for it,' he explained to me.

'From who?' I asked out of curiosity. Johnny looked up from devouring his bowl:

'Old Mister Wu. Who do you think?' He winked at me, his mouth full.

'The old bugger still keeps a supply. Scarcity, my arse!'

I looked from the untouched bowl on the table to Zhang and back again. Isn't he going to eat? I thought. Old Zhang kept muttering the same words out while stroking his wounded arm. It sounded like 'Neeta, neeta.'

'Where have you been?' he asked me.

'Nowhere.'

'Haven't seen you in a while.'

'Or Li?' I said.

'Or Li,' said Johnny, still eating.

'Are you not surprised?'

'Li does not surprise me anymore,' he said.

I did not understand what was meant by this.

'Père Olivier, the priest was taken away,' I said quietly.

'Yes, I heard.'

'How?' I said.

'Talk!' he said, showing his fingers in the shape of a talking mouth. He carried on eating.

'Uncle Zhang, your rice will go cold and lumpy.'

Zhang appeared oblivious to everything around him except the fire's blaze.

'How's your dog?' Johnny asked me.

'Misha is fine,' I said.

'Mind her,' he said. 'There is talk...of going back.'

'Going back?'

'To killing and eating dogs – food.'

I recoiled in horror...Misha? Food? I felt sick.

'Supplies of some food are getting scarce now, we're told.'

Misha is food? I thought. It is all eating – eat this, eat that... fish, meat, fruit, eat everything. Eat everything that lives. Is nothing forbidden? What's this forbidden fruit the Christian Bible talks of? And Tang mentioning oranges to Pere O? It all lives – all except bread! Bread is not alive, is it? But what of Père O's bread? Is it alive, too? He said it was. That it is flesh and blood.

I looked at the rice getting cold on the table and my hunger went away. In truth I did not ever want to eat anything again, even Père O's bread. So I blurted it out:

'Johnny, did you tell on Li?'

'Tell what?

'And Père O?'

'What are you saying?' he answered with his mouth full. I waited for an answer. Johnny placed his chopsticks down and chewed his last mouthful carefully.

'Li was getting indoctrinated by that *Laowai*. It was bad medicine.'

Old Zhang groaned even louder, 'Neeta, Neeta,' as the flames illuminated his face.

'Johnny, did you tell?'

'She was seeing that *Laowai* too much for her own good.'

'My sister?' I shouted, sensing tears coming.

'My friend, the *Laowai*?' I shouted, my face getting hot. The fire was rising now in the fireplace.

'You told Tang,' I said low, not shouting now, my voice getting weak with emotion.

'Anita, Anita,' old Zhang was chanting.

'You are an informer!' I said finally, with a tremor in my voice and tears falling out. Johnny looked at me and said angrily and slowly:

'Li is pregnant...and the *Laowai* is the father.'

I was stopped in my tracks. What? Li is pregnant? But she is not even married, how could this be? I looked blankly at him. Old Zhang kept on chanting in the corner.

'Yes,' said Johnny then. 'Your sister has gotten herself pregnant and the *Laowai* is the father. Why else was she visiting him in the evenings?'

'What are you saying, Johnny?'

'That you will soon be an uncle,' Johnny said.

I looked over at Zhang, Johnny's uncle. Then it all made sense.

'But why did you turn her in?' I said.

Johnny kept on chewing rice. He did not answer. I stood there in the middle of their floor, dazed and confused, angry yet still unsure. I felt like crying.

Johnny finished eating now, lay the bowl down on the table, and stood up.

'Li and the *Laowai* were practising a forbidden religion,' he said, grabbing his cap and he walked out the door, slamming it behind.

Old Zhang ceased his muttering once the door had shut. He turned to me with his hairy face. 'Sit down. I must relate something to you. 'He patted the stool next to him. I sat facing the warm fire. I tried explaining my story to Zhang.

'My sister has been taken for no reason. My friend the *Laowai* priest, also.'

Zhang squeezed his bad arm as if it were causing him bother.

'I, too, am cursed,' he said. Not this again, I thought.

'Johnny also, I believe,' he said after.

'You know, Tang, our village commander?' he went on. I nodded.

'Tang is from here.' He indicated the surrounding area. 'Tang, however, is *very* clever. He has read much – much more than I can ever know. Bah! I could never read, but a long time back I, too, had some knowledge.

'I was young once. I, too, had passions. Blood red ones; both political and amorous. You see I was a Communist – once! I became one when I worked in Shanghai in my youth. I went to all the meetings, listened to the debates. I could never read but I heard. And I experienced first-hand feudalism and capitalism. I organised workers in Shanghai – would you like some tea?' I said no to this. 'Well, I would like to drink.' He stood and walked to a press and took out a jug. He bit off the cork and poured a cup with his good hand. 'Good. There is some left.'

'Oh, I know all the arguments for Communism, alright. In love I was, too. A young girl, she was. She worked with me in the city. She was so pretty.' He stopped for a moment looking intoxicated, thinking to himself. Then he rambled on:

'I worked on the docks in Shanghai. Heavy work. Tough, thirsty work. In the evenings she would call to my lodgings and we would talk politics and plot the future world.' He shook his head laughing at this.

'She tried to teach me to read all those works I wish I had read. She would also bring me wine to sate the thirst.   ..I had a ferocious thirst...' He looked at the cup he held.

'...And we would be happy. She seemed magical, even to be able to work magic. I cannot explain...'

Zhang paused then and placed his good hand out, palms facing down, and studied it.

'Is it shaking?' he asked.

'I cannot tell,' I said.

'It sure feels like,' he said. Then he continued:

'I have never felt so happy as when I was with her. Just being in her company, her presence, I felt such harmony.'

He examined his hand again.

'Is it really possible?' he whispered.

'What?' I said.

He did not answer but continued:

'I was so in love with her. I know I was young then, I know. I do not know if she felt the same but we were becoming close.' He spoke with emotion.

'She could read. Read to me all the literature so I could spout it all off. And I did. She was trying to teach me to read.'

'Where is this girl now?' I said.

'Dead,' he said.

I said nothing then.

'Yes,' he said, holding the cup of rice wine. 'Her name was Anita.'

'Rumour was spread that I got her pregnant. She could not take it – the dirty looks, the stares – remember it is different for women now as well as then. So, one night she hanged herself.'

'Was she pregnant?'

'I do not know, exactly,' he said. 'Or who it was that spread the rumour – either some jealous comrades or our class enemies in the Shanghai establishment – there were many in both those camps. I never found out.'

He took a swig of the drink. 'Had I known I would most definitely have killed them.' He downed the cup of wine.

'That ended me with Shanghai. I returned home to fish The River, as I had started in life.'

'And the curse?' I said. 'The one you always talk about.'

'Is that not proof enough?' he said. 'I don't know.' He paused, reflecting on what to say. 'I think she cursed me,' he said then.

'How so? She must have loved you?'

'The rumour I spoke about also included it was me boasted I got her pregnant,' he said, tears coming to his eyes.

'I never did anything of the kind.'

'That is so horrible,' I said.

'Precisely. People can be wicked. Either I was carrying a curse, or she cursed me with her last breath, for she never allowed me to explain my story. Ever after, women avoided me like the plague. Johnny has elements of being cursed, too.'

'Johnny?'

'Yes. With girls,' he explained. 'It may be a family curse. Some bad luck.'

'And Tang?'

'Oh, Tang,' said Zhang. 'All he ever learned about politics he got from me.'

'What?' I was truly amazed.

'Yes. When he was younger he called over every day to learn about life in the big city and I professed my knowledge to him, of communism as well of course. I even gave him all the literature I brought back from Shanghai – no good to me then or now – and he devoured it all.'

Zhang laughed. 'He swallowed it all, hook, line, and sinker!' Then he downed another cup of wine. 'The Party Line! It is rumoured he is even Moscow-trained. And I started it all.'

'He is smart,' I said. 'This I know.'

'Smart?' he laughed again. 'Just look at it all now...they are like headless chickens. Tang is...'

He refused to finish. Then said,

'I'm sorry, kid.' Shaking his head smiling, a stewed grin on his stubbled face. 'I'm just a cynic.'

'A sin...?' I tried to say the word.

'Now you.' He pointed at me, still holding his cup. 'You must not allow people to persecute your sister over this. This is not of her making. Johnny is blind. 'He shook his head. 'He is...'

Again he did not finish. He walked to the window saying nothing more. He simply stared outside. After a while, I realised he had finished, so I said farewell and left.

A t midday the village assembled in the wide street, waiting. I stood on a sidewalk gangway for a better view, watching it all beside Zhu. I watched as everybody, people I knew, people Li knew, all began to gather there on the street. The day was overcast and dull, the sun rested this day behind grey clouds that enveloped the whole skyline. It was warm, though.

Firstly a column of Red Army marched into the space and lined up at attention. The red flag was raised in the usual fashion and the villagers saluted.

There was a silence for a short while. Some people murmured quietly among themselves. Then, some movement among the crowd, a stirring. Something was happening. Heads were directed west towards Mister Xi's home at the top of the village. I looked and I saw the prisoners being led to the street by soldiers. There was a collective gasp from all the people there looking on. There was Mister Xi, Père O, and lastly, I spotted Li. My heart leapt as soon as I saw her there being marched along in file behind the other two   prisoners. I watched closely. I had not set eyes on my sister since the morning they came to take her away. She seemed so weak there, Li who was normally so strong and solid as a rock for me.

Père O was standing tall and upright as he walked along.

Mister Xi walked proudly, bowing to those who clapped as he went by, as if he were still the mayor. Many there still regarded him as such, such was the length of time he had been village Elder, and then mayor.

Once they reached the centre of the wide street they were marshalled over to the side, all three of them lined up beside each other. There was unease amongst the crowd of villagers standing around. They formed a ring around the open space where the three were and where the army lined up. Then someone called out, 'Here he comes.' The name 'Tang' was mentioned by almost everybody there.

Tang walked briskly into view, holding papers in his hand, appearing very business-like.

'This won't last long,' some old man said.

'It'll be over in time for tea,' said another.

The guards saluted Tang, who acknowledged them, then he bowed courteously to the three prisoners. Only Xi bowed back. Père O stood tall in the middle of the three, while Li's shoulders looked slumped. I was worried for her. Tang turned around to the assembled village. He raised an arm for attention. People elbowed each other.

'He wants to speak.'

'Listen up.'

'Tang.'

Tang then spoke. But we couldn't all hear him. He spoke low, not loudly, so that everybody shut up and all strained to hear him. I missed the first things he said because of this, but gradually my ears could just about hear him.

'They are brought here before me on charges – very serious charges. So much so, that in keeping with the democratic principles of socialism, I want to hear this trial here in public, in broad daylight, before their fellow citizens. You, good people of Zhaoui should consider yourselves privileged not to be here before the law, to be exemplary citizens of the new China being fought for at the present time all around us. Once victory is achieved and we have the People's' Republic, you will feel humbled and honoured to be full participants in its daily life. The Revolution has begun, there is no turning back. The old regime is finished. It is just a matter of time. History waits for no-one.

'I propose to hear these allegations made against the three prisoners standing here before you. And following this process I will give my judgements. The prisoners will be questioned in public and given the opportunity to defend themselves.

'I want to thank the soldiers of the People's' Liberation Army who are here performing their duty on our behalf.'

When he said this the villagers clapped their hands for a bit. Tang carried on:

'So, first we must identify the prisoners. Prisoners…' He looked at the three.

'When I call your name out please step forward.' Tang then opened the sheet of paper he carried:

'Xi-lo, step forward,

'Li-tan, step forward,

'Jacques Olivier, step forward.'

When he said Père O's name, he sounded so strange trying to pronounce it, the people laughed. All three stepped forward one pace in line.

'Let us now hear the charges,' said Tang. A Red Army soldier on Tang's prompting read aloud from a list. His voice was shrill and tinny.

'Xi-lo, you are accused of misleading the people of Zhaoui, of exploitation, of multiple incidents of corruption.'

Mister Xi for the first time appeared lost for words. He shook his head in disbelief.

'But I am innocent,' he protested.

The soldier continued, 'Li-tan you are accused of repeatedly taking instructions in an activity forbidden, of reading banned reactionary literature, of conspiring with enemies of the people.'

Li, who appeared pale and delicate, stood upright and said loudly, 'That is nonsense.'

'You received instruction in a foreign religion despite it being forbidden,' the soldier shouted at her.

'What evidence is there?' she said back.

'Pleading not guilty,' said Tang.

'The *Laowai*, Jacques Olivier,' the soldier said with difficulty. 'Is accused of a forbidden practice and of promoting this to others in the village of Zhaoui despite it being prohibited and also of subversive activity.'

'My faith is my life. And worth much more,' said Père O, clearing his throat. Some villagers laughed at his response, not really understanding.

'We shall see,' said Tang, again speaking low so we strained to hear. I do not know why Tang spoke in that low voice considering he could give big booming speeches with ease.

He then said, 'We are here to listen to these allegations, you to answer for yourselves, and I to decide. But the people can also form their own judgements. As I said, I believe in being democratic.'

The villagers then began to mutter amongst themselves, and nudged each other with glances exchanged. They were truly expecting something big, something extraordinary this day.

Suddenly, the Red Army soldier shouted at Xi, 'Who elected or appointed you mayor of Zhaoui?'

Mister Xi, taken by surprise at first, came to, and answered,

'Why the authorities!'

'What authorities?' the soldier demanded out loud.

'Nanking,' said Xi, with a grin.

The people smiled at this answer. They had a traditional respect for Nanking's authority. They thought Mister Xi was wonderful in all his dealings.

'On what basis? That you would spy for them? Be their agent in all things?' the soldier continued. I looked at Tang, who was expressionless throughout this.

'No,' considered Mister Xi. 'Because, I suppose, because I was previously the village Elder.'

'How were you that? Who elected you?' said the soldier straight away.

'My father was Elder before me.'

'And who elected him?' said the soldier, placing his hands on his hips facing the crowd.

'You mean you inherited the role of Elder without election or popular appointment? The Kuomintang put you in as mayor to do their corrupt bidding. I have no more to say here.'

Mister Xi thought his behaviour was perfectly normal. He was usually so very sharp in his dealings and words. Some in the crowd started muttering amongst themselves.

'That's right, who actually appointed him?'

'Who chose you?'

'Corruption at its finest,' went on the soldier.

The trial had actually already begun and no-one really knew it. Questioning by that Red Army soldier had in fact kicked it off. We slowly copped this.

'Do you not get a percentage of every private business in Zhaoui? Free treatment everywhere despite being well able to pay?'

Mister Xi seemed dumbfounded. The short soldier then strutted around an embarrassed Mister Xi, showing him up.

'Priest – do you practice the forbidden Roman mass ritual?' The soldier then shouted at Père O. Père O looked to be surprised by the sudden invective. He was caught unawares.

'The Mass is normal for a priest,' he replied.

'Normal, you say? You practise it then?

Père O did not answer straight away.

'It is forbidden to do so,' said the soldier.

'Did you instruct any people of Zhaoui in this forbidden religion?'

Père O did not answer.

'You are indeed a subversive,' said the short soldier.

After this preliminary questioning, it started again. The crowd were thoroughly engrossed. We had never witnessed such a thing in Zhaoui before. Even Zhang was present in the crowd somewhere, I saw him. The three prisoners, by their differing stances, told varying stories: Père O, tall and upright, Mister Xi, fidgety and confused, Li, a determined face, but slouched shoulders, displaying nerves, I believe. I knew her so well.

'Priest – you admit to practising your mass for your own ends...did you do so for others in the village?'

Again, Père O did not answer.

'You are a subversive, priest? – I put it to you.'

'My faith has subverted even the greatest of empires,' Père O said.

The short soldier stood back and gestured to Père O as if to show him up. Some of the crowd gasped and began to jeer Père O.

'Even your comrade Stalin in Russia has asked, "How many battalions has the pope?"' said Père O, trying to be heard. 'I can give you an answer...' he said.

When he said this I wondered if this pope of Père O's was sending an army at this very moment? I imagined I could hear them in the distance, in the nearby hills maybe. Would they put a stop to all this? But I could not hear what he spoke after, for the crowd became even more restless at this. The soldier smiled and said no more.

To Li then this short soldier demanded:

'Did you receive instructions in a forbidden activity – a Mass? Practise the banned Roman faith? Read banned books?'

'This is ridiculous. When is it forbidden to read?' she said.

'Certain literature is forbidden,' he said.

'No,' answered Li directly.

'No? Really?' The soldier again stood back to let the people view Li.

'Li-tan, did you accept instruction in the forbidden Roman Mass?'

'No.'

I watched Tang, who appeared to scrutinise everything.

'You have been seen entering the home of the *Laowai* on numerous occasions. Explain this then?'

Li looked at Tang. 'Do I have to?'

Tang nodded, gravely.

'I had business with him – the priest.'

'Business?' shouted the soldier with the sharp voice.

'My business is none of your business,' said Li.

'Be careful of selfish individualism,' shouted the soldier.

'It is personal,' Li said.

'But this may have a bearing on your fate,' said Tang, sounding reasonable.

Li said nothing more to this.

'So it seems both of you prefer silence than answers to pertinent questions,' said the short soldier then.

'Silence signifies guilt,' he added. 'We have established the *Laowai* priest practises his forbidden religion on his own, that Li-tan has been seen visiting this priest on occasion and cannot explain why.'

The short soldier strutted in the centre of the space surrounded by the assembled people who watched earnestly, some looked puzzled – this type of thing had never happened before. Tang stood observing all, while the three, my own Li included, faced him. I went down closer to the action as I found it difficult to hear both Tang and Li who spoke low. I weaved my way through the crowd to sit on the ground before the front row with a perfect view of everything.

Mister Xi must have then got tired on his feet, for he sat on the ground in his position facing Tang. One of the guards went to butt him with a rifle to get him up but Tang waved his arm to say it was alright, so Xi continued to sit.

Tang then spoke: 'Who here has seen Li-tan visit the priest?'

'Two from the village saw her – more than one. And saw literature in her house/'

'What literature?' said Tang.

'Banned Roman literature.'

Then Li spoke up: 'You have lent me books, comrade,' she addressed Tang.

Tang looked stumped. Instead of words he reached for his pack of cigarettes and lit one. Everyone looked in Tang's direction.

'I gave you literature to read about the revolution,' he said calmly.

People gasped at this – 'She can read!' was heard coming from the crowd.

'The priest also gave her books,' said the short soldier sharply.

'How so?' said Tang.

'Witnesses.'

'Witnesses?' said Tang. 'Come forward then,' he said firmly.

At this, the crowd stepped backwards in unison and looked around. Confusion was evident all round. Then he walked up – Johnny. The crowd seemed dismayed. They stirred restlessly.

Tang addressed him directly. 'You are the accuser?'

'I have seen the religious books in her house,' said Johnny. 'Books such as the Christian Bible and others.'

'Subversive,' shouted the soldier at Père O.

Tang held his cigarette in one hand, listening.

'You like to read?' he asked Li. 'And not just mine?'

Li bit her lip tight. Eventually she answered, 'I am learning how to pray...'

'There's more,' said Johnny, agitated.

'...For somebody.' Li finished her sentence, but no one could hear her – the crowd were busy whispering, 'The girl can read?'

Tang lifted an eyebrow at Johnny.

'Yes,' Johnny continued, 'She is carrying a child in her...and this priest is the father. 'He pointed out both Li and Père O. The crowd sighed loudly with amazement. Tang inhaled his cigarette and said gravely.

'That is no crime.'

'They are immoral,' said Johnny.

'Johnny,' said Li, her hand to her mouth.

'You and the *Laowai*,' Johnny said to her.

'It is no crime,' said Tang emphatically.

By now the crowd had become uneasy and agitated. They began to make noise.

'Are you pregnant?' the soldier asked Li.

Li at first stared at the ground, then slowly wiped her face of perspiration, brushed her hair with her hand. She stood forward and spoke:

'I have often seen when a man has a woman...or women...he is a big man. But for a woman to have even one man before marriage, she is a whore in society.'

'Do you admit it?' asked the soldier.

Li continued as if she hadn't been interrupted: 'She is a whore in the eyes of everyone – except that man. Then that man joins society in calling other women whores who will not go with him, who he cannot have.'

Johnny looked at Li. 'Whore,' he said.

Li bit her lip and trembled.

'Are you the father of Li-tan's child?' the soldier asked Père O.

'Enough,' said Tang.

Père O said nothing. Li seemed to look over at him with appealing eyes. I saw Père O nod slightly.

'This man is not the father,' said Li, pointing at Père O to her right.

'Then you *are* pregnant,' said Johnny, 'Whore'

'It is true I visited Père Olivier,' said Li. 'It is true I received religious instructions from him.' She looked at Johnny then. 'You were away fighting. We heard your letters and what war is like. 'She placed her hand on Johnny's forearm. 'Yes, I prayed with Père Olivier. But I prayed for you. For you Johnny...to return safely home from the war. I was only learning to pray for your sake...to pray for *you*!'

Johnny jerked away his arm and turned away. His face had changed – like he was embarrassed or ashamed. The crowd murmured out loud at all this. Somewhere among the crowd I thought I heard Zhang say, 'cursed again' – somewhere I think, though I might have been imagining it. Then Tang took control of the situation.

'We have heard enough,' he said.

'I am convinced of the guilt on the charges mentioned, of Xi-lo and of Jacques Olivier. I therefore have no choice but to order them to be shot as punishment.'

The crowd clapped him for saying this.

'Shot forthwith,' he said then.

'The case of Li-tan is different, and more complex. I must have time to consider a while longer and I shall give my judgement tomorrow early. For women, getting pregnant is not a crime.'

Before he called the end of the trial, the Red Army soldiers had marched away with Mister Xi and Père Olivier, while two guards led Li off in a different direction.

That was it, then. At first I couldn't quite take it all in. I refused to accept the judgement, thinking it a mistake on Tang's part. Li would be home again soon, fetching water and making supper. I would be back visiting Père O. The whole trial was a farce and couldn't be real.

The villagers slowly dispersed to go about their business. Of course some groups lingered, huddled around chatting gossip about what they just witnessed. This would not go away, I knew. I was truly shocked and educated at the same time by what I heard and could only wonder what the rest of the village thought. I remained standing there, the very last to leave the street. Zhu's mother had dragged him off once Li had finished speaking, Zhu's eyes fixed on me as he was led away.

The clouds got thicker and darker overhead, rain looked imminent. Suddenly, the sound of fire   crackers rang out from behind the houses – four shots. A man came running up,

'They've shot Mayor Xi and the *Laowai*,' he said excitedly.

The people gasped audibly. I did not believe him.

'Pop, pop each, in the back of the head,' he said, placing his forefinger to his head and pretending to shoot.

'No? So soon?' somebody said.

'Pop, pop – I saw it all,' he said again, mimicking the sound of gunshots.

More shook their heads, others said,

'They deserved it – traitors.'

'Oh, yeah,' another said. 'How so?'

I bawled my eyes out, standing there. Père O was my friend and teacher. He hadn't done anything wrong, not deliberately. He talked to God and taught us about God. Was this wrong? Even if you did not believe it all, was it wrong?

And Mister Xi? He had been here forever, I thought. Forever and ever. I thought he would always be. Then I remembered Tang's 'No turning back' remark.

The soldiers then shouted at us to go home, lifting their weapons in emphasis. We walked away, looking behind us at the scene of the day's happenings. This was a truly horrible day. I must have cried all the way back home. I was alone now, I realised then. Père O was dead, shot in the head. Li was taken away from me. How could I cope? The rain clouds filled the space overhead and the first droplets fell on the dusty street. It felt cooler, too. Much cooler for mid-June. It was a bad summer.

The combination of the sudden darkness in the sky, the rain and the deserted street, made the village seem eerie to me as I walked home sobbing my eyes out for Li and Père O. I did not want to ever see Johnny again, or even old Zhang...

So I walked home in tears, but if anyone saw me they wouldn't know, because the rain came down heavier now. It seemed as if not only the sky had turned grey but the air also; a perpetual darkness covered the village. Arriving at the house I saw the first one – the first sign that I was in danger and should be careful. It couldn't have been a joke, it was too gruesome. It looked like a dragon's head on a long neck. A shape of a head, it was a skull impaled on a stake standing before our house. An animal skull – a dog's!

I took hold of it in my hands and I flung it away to land on wet dirt. I felt paralysed for a moment, then it immediately dawned on me. I rushed round the back to check on Misha. The woodshed door looked unopened, untampered with. I opened it. There she was lying in the corner, her tail slowly coming to life in tiny movements. She was nervous, like with strangers. Yes she was nervous about something. I could tell.

'It's me, girl,' I said to reassure her.

I sat in the woodshed with her as the rain poured down now outside, and I thought of Li.

I was awakened by the thundering of the rain on the thin rooftop of the little woodshed and the wind rattling around the yard. Misha wagged her tail to see me awake at last. My first thoughts were about the day just passed. I thought of Li, then of Père O and his death. I still couldn't believe it all happened. And Mister Xi? Could it actually be possible they were dead?

I could not rest any longer. It was dark by now. I did not even know if it was the same day or how long I slept. I felt hungry. I needed food and knew I couldn't rely on Zhu any longer – or Johnny!

I decided to go to Tang to plead with him to free Li so that life could go back to normal for us. I wanted it to be like it used to be. I left Misha tied in the woodshed and left to go to Tang. It was a wet and windy night but as I entered the street I saw a crowd going towards the River. There was a hustle and bustle about the place. What was going on? I noticed it was only the menfolk. They were loud and all going in the same direction.

I walked the opposite direction towards the army encampment on the outskirts of the village. There, two guards were on duty. They asked me where did I think I was going?

'I need to see Commander Tang,' I said.

They glanced at each other then at me.

'On what business?'

'I need to see him.'

'Go home, kid, the Commander is busy.'

'But I must see him.'

'Can't you go home? He's busy.'

'Piss off,' said the second guard.

I walked away but not back. I knew where Tang's tent was at the end of the last row. So I doubled back round by Wu's store to the backyards of the huts and houses on this side of the village and approached the encampment of tents from the exposed side. Once again, there were strange dialects and cooking smells coming from inside the different tents. Some were even playing music in their tents. Music I did not quite recognise.

In the dark I located Tang's and undid the flap to go inside. I did not know what I would say but I wanted to have him release Li. Once in, I saw nothing except the lamp lighting the inside. On his table lay scattered sheets of paper and notes everywhere. There was no sign of him about, but I knew he was there because of the blue smoke filling the space. I heard a cough from the very back. Tang lay on his cot smoking a cigarette. Despite the fog of smoke I could make him out there in his cot; one hand lay by his side holding the cigarette, the other was placed on his temple. He was thinking to himself. I approached the bed. He must have sensed me, for he quickly leapt to his feet and reached for the holster which was suspended from the cot rails. Before he took out his revolver he recognised me:

'You! How did you get in here? What do you want?'

I felt tongue-tied and afraid, but slowly spoke.

'I want Li. I want my sister back.'

'Oh,' said Tang, taking a final drag on his cigarette before stepping on it. 'I see. I understand now.'

There was a blue haze of smoke surrounding the lamp.

'Let me tell you,' he said. 'I have had to pretend to the village – and my troops – that I was seriously considering her fate. In truth, I knew straight away what I would do.'

I looked quizzically at him, without speaking.

'I am going to release her, let her free. On the grounds that the *Laowai* deliberately misled her.'

I felt like saying, you deliberately killed my friend, that *Laowai*, but was too scared to.

'She is having a baby' was all I could say. Tang looked at me, smiled, and said:

'No, she's not. She's carrying *my* baby.'

He reached for the pack of cigarettes on his table and lit another one up. I noticed the pack was not the Tiger brand he favoured, but Lucky Strike, which Père Olivier kept a supply of for gifts and bribery. I looked straight at him.

'What do you mean?'

'Yes, I'll end this charade and let her go tomorrow. She's carrying my child.'

'Your child?'

Tang sat down on his cot. His collar was undone and the buttons on his tunic were open halfway down. He continued to smoke.

'I've loved your sister all my life. You don't remember me but I used to try to court her when we were younger. Before old Zhang introduced me to a much bigger love than women: politics and the revolution.'

He went on, 'I am for the people but I am also of the people – in short, I'm a man – with needs, and Li is a woman – with needs!'

He looked at my puzzled face.

'Oh, you're too young to see what I mean now. When you're older you'll understand. You will lose innocence, too.

'Johnny put two and two together and got three and a half. Old Zhang would be horrified. Lao Tzu would be horrified. Karl Marx would love it!' Tang smiled.

'Why kill the *Laowai*?' I said then.

He sucked on his cigarette, coughed a bit, then:

'He was breaking the law and I had to take action.'

'He did no wrong.'

'He broke the law. The law is the law and must be obeyed – especially in times of revolution, otherwise chaos and defeat.'

'He was my friend.'

'I'm sorry.'

I lowered my head to cry again. Tang stood up and placed his hand on my shoulder.

'I had to keep control in the village, to set an example early into our liberation of your village. He was also accused of being a subversive, remember?'

I looked up at him twice.

'Please,' I said, 'Li.'

He sprung up and grabbed and buckled the revolver belt around his waist.

'Come on,' he said curtly 'Let's find Li. I've made my decision.'

I followed him out of the tent and along the lined tents past the two guards, who looked startled by the sight of me with Tang. We marched in the direction of Xi's old home.

'Where are we going?' I asked.

'To the prisoners' quarters,' said Tang.

I never knew where they kept Li, or Père Olivier, for that matter, I just assumed they were in some army tent. Mister Xi was detained in his own house, that we all knew. House arrest, it was called. Now, I realised that all three were held in Xi's house. It was so obvious.

One guard on the front door saluted Tang.

'Where are the others?' Tang demanded.

'Comrade Commander, they have gone to check on the commotion in the village,' said the soldier on guard.

'Commotion?' said Tang, 'What is this?'

'It seems there is rioting and a mob down in the village.'

'What? Why was I not told?'

'The men went to investigate first – before disturbing you, Comrade Commander. You left orders not to disturb you tonight.'

'Open the door,' said Tang impatiently.

'Yes, Comrade Commander.'

The guard unlocked the door of Xi's old house. I followed Tang inside. It was dark. The hallway was an abyss of black to be negotiated using our hands to navigate. Not even a candle lighting.

Poor Li, I thought, was this where she really was kept? Tang flicked his cigarette lighter on and led the way, calling Li's name.

'Li-tan, it's only me. You're going to be freed. I'm letting you go home.'

I looked around me in the little light visible and wondered at Mister Xi's big house. There was carpet, and lamps...and pictures. Such luxury in our small village. No-one had ever probably seen inside Xi's house before – except Mister Wu, who was his cousin, and Wu's wife, who was his cook. Tang went on calling for Li but no answer came. I called out, too:

'Li, it's alright now.'

I noticed Tang had entered one room and the tiny flicker of light went out. I followed him in. Tang was on his knees, he had dropped his lighter. I felt around, picked it up, and flicked the switch on awkwardly, letting it fall a couple of times.

'Oh, no' Tang was sobbing 'Oh no, oh no.'

I saw first her feet dangling in front of me. Then the rest: Li was hanging from a chord. Dead.

'Oh no,' Tang was saying.

I felt the enormous weight of the world on me that instant. I wanted to cry but couldn't. My heart was bursting yet felt too heavy to explode. My head panicked. I looked around me.

'I love you, Li,' I heard Tang saying, 'I love you.'

'I admit it now…It's my child. Johnny was wrong – not the priest – me…I'm the father.'

I looked at Tang in horror.

I touched her feet suspended there. Her body was cold, lifeless. My sister, my only sister. Then, slowly, I backed away out of the room.

I kept on slowly walking out of the house just as two soldiers came running in. In the darkness they didn't see me. I overheard one say to Tang:

'Comrade Commander, there is a mob ransacking the church and house of the *Laowai* priest. What are your orders, Comrade Commander?'

I left then, walking up the street in the night. The rain had stopped but the wind remained, billowing gusts through the village like I imagined phantoms. Stars winked above in an ink night sky, the moon was hidden by a wisp of cloud.

As I came nearer the house I heard the noise of the mob and sound of breaking wood and smashing glass. I was now truly alone. By myself. I would have to survive. Then I thought of Misha. She was mine. But for how long? It would be only a matter of time when Chen would be lucky and have her. If not him then someone else. Everyone had warned me to get rid of Misha. I could not let her fall into Chen's hands, or anyone else's for that matter. I would take her down to the River and dispose of her in a decent manner, that's all. Poor thing.

I walked numb through the village that lonely night, my eyes blinded with tears. I felt myself invisible and could go anywhere unnoticed. The noise got louder as I went round the back of the house to the woodshed. I opened and entered, found her asleep, and woke her. She was hungry, as was I, yet she greeted me with her customary warmth and love.

'Here, Misha.' I took her by the rope and we crept away by the backs of the houses in the direction of the stream that flowed out to the River. We followed it, passing the long hut used by Père Olivier as a church. We heard the mob inside breaking it to pieces, his small house, too. A noise of destruction. The sounds must have carried across the river. I could make out Chen's voice among the throng. Misha was a timid dog and was nervous. We crept by the noise and the breaking, huddled down, each footstep gauged and calculated like it was when in the Hills over that uneven terrain. I pulled Misha in stops and starts. Each movement could have us spotted by one of the mob. Then, some movement caused us to stop in our tracks. A cough. I heard it. Just as we reached the high uncut grass flanking the stream to the rear of the huts and homes of Zhaoui. Someone was having a cigarette. Probably taking a quick break while all the destruction was taking place around Père O's. At first I froze. Then, scared Misha would bark, I muzzled her with my fingers, in a grip.

Whoever it was, was breathing hard as if breathless. Then a darkness appeared in the ground over us – a shadow...among the shadows. He was standing on the mound right above us. I could even smell the fumes from his cigarette. We had to move onwards out of his reach but it would be awkward with Misha, or else lie low till he went away again. The wheezy breathing stopped. I turned around and looked up. It was dark but I could sense someone was there. Were they waiting for us to move? Could they know? Another cough. It was as if I could recognise its sound, something familiar about it.

I continued to muzzle Misha, who now began to act scared. What was it she sensed? Slowly, I crawled a bit further, at the same time leading Misha with difficulty. We managed to get out from being directly under him, but he was still there I could sense. Misha began trembling now but my grip around her mouth prevented any unwanted sound from her.

'Easy now, Misha,' I whispered softly.

She kicked a bit at this, a sort of silent struggle. It would be better if I never had her now, I thought to myself. Beyond us the noise of rioting. Was the village now ransacking Père O's house? Where was Tang and the army?

Another cough. And we froze again. Just then the night got clearer. The cloudy veil had left the moon to shine again. It shimmered silver light to places which were black before. Misha and I were still in the shadows, though, below the mound in the grass. I felt brave enough to stick my head up to look. Keeping my body flat, I parted the tall grass stems and spied upwards. I saw him. Sitting there away from the ruckus holding his hands around his knees – Chen!

I knew Misha smelled his presence, for she kicked her hind legs to escape my grip. She could give the whole game away, while I could lay low all night. I peeked up to check again. Chen wasn't moving. He could remain there for hours, I thought. Our only hope was to gradually crawl away. But now the clear moon illuminated everything, and Misha kept struggling, so I was sure we would be discovered.

Slowly, I crawled through grass and muck on one elbow forward while tugging Misha's rope and holding my grip on her nozzle with my other hand. She seemed to intuitively realise I was helping her, for she complied in moving forward with me. Sometimes she'd make a whimper, but too low to arouse any suspicion. The usual night sounds of toad croaking filled the air as well as the noise coming from Père O's.

Then a noise from above: Chen began speaking, or so I thought. We were rumbled? But no intelligible sounds came out. Instead just a singing. He was speaking some strange song, a kind of wailing. He sounded like a half-wit. This was the opportunity I needed to move faster along on my stomach, dragging myself with my left arm and elbow while pulling Misha with my right, all the time keeping her down low in the high grass beneath the mound where sat Chen.

'Easy now, girl,' I said.

So slowly, one move at a time, each movement focused as if I were climbing a steep mountain and each step spelling danger, we went along one foot at a time, one step, I focused all my thoughts, all my world, on that one step, a wrong footing could be it. In a while, we had eventually cleared the danger area and found ourselves heading down the slopes towards The River. I had one more duty to perform, a terrible one, yes, but I had deemed it necessary and best.

'Don't worry, girl,' I said to her.

The night hid us as I led her down to the river bank. 'Come on, girl.'

In the darkness I anchored her rope to a heavy rock by the river's edge. I hugged her one last time, with tears of sadness and anger. Slowly I reached out and picked up a stone to kill her with. Better this way than the alternative, I thought. Misha's eyes looking beggingly into mine with her head tilted to one side.

Just then a ferocious red light appeared from behind, illuminating the water – flames. They were burning Père Olivier's church. A loud cheer rang out from behind us. I heard gunshots, too. The army must be keeping order at last.

Something stirred in the water in the background. I could just about see it now with the light from the flames. It was a skiff, a sampan. It was tied loosely with plenty of slack. Old Zhang's skiff was berthed just behind us on the water. My thoughts changed then, as if I had come to. I put the stone down.

'Come on, girl,' I said. 'Let's go.'

We waded out to the sampan and climbed aboard. I had to literally drag Misha up by the rope but she clambered up on her own once she got a grip. I had learned how to sail on The River. I untied the mooring and pushed off, manning the tiller to navigate. I couldn't see a thing in front except what the blazing fire was lighting up for us, but I knew the direction of Shanghai – down river!

A fortunate gust of wind suddenly helped us blow off and we were on our way, like the parting kiss of breath from a lover. Red sparks like fire moths were carried along with smoke out on this gust. Something else landed on the deck as well though – flakes of paper. Some burnt pages scattered in front of me with the accompanying smell of smoke. I went to brush them away and noticed some print on one of these brown-stained, burnt, crisp leaves. It read:

PARADISE LOST
John Milton

It was *the* book that Père Olivier was always reading from, alongside his Christian Bible. I did not look back then at my native Zhaoui. I remember swallowing my throat filled with such emotion, and holding back tears, I sailed on into the darkness, leaving the noise, the flames, and the village behind us and slowly disappeared into the shade of The River at night with its soft rippling water before us beckoning us on towards a new life. A sort of baptism in place of one I never had.

The Conversation

Fr Kiely strolled towards the windows, his fist still cupped. He had something to say.

'We – the Company – always strive to cater for the temporal as well as the spiritual needs of our people.'

Père Olivier's eyebrows lifted a smattering at this.

Christ, he's a cool one, thought Kiely. He had noticed the scars along the wrists...they're healing pretty fast, too.

'You do the Exercises?'

'Done and dusted.'

'Let's not say dusted. They're living exercises, written down by St Ignatius but primarily for practice – you practice them as the spirit takes you – Spiritual Exercises.'

Suicide ideation I believe is the contemporary term...I wonder?

Fr Kiely went on. 'Jacques, you are known to practice the so-called Eastern meditations? Yoga and such?'

Père Olivier nodded assent.

Fat lot of good they did you then.

'Not that there's anything considered wrong with that. In fact I believe our American Fathers are taking a great interest in Eastern methods of reflection and contemplation as part of spiritual retreats – though we do have our own Exercises as dictated by St Ignatius.'

Père Olivier again nodded.

'You've visited?

'Father?'

'The East? India? Tibet?'

'There was a war on till recently, Father, a world war.'

'Oh, yes, you would be too young. But you speak Chinese?'

'Some Mandarin,' Olivier corrected.

'Ah the confounded Orient. So many tongues and dialects.'

'The Fall of Babel,' said Olivier grinning.

Fr Kiely glared, 'Quite, yes, quite.'

We're sending you off there, Father Jacques Olivier SJ. Before this month is out.

'Our Lord fell three times, Father, don't forget,' he said on his way towards the door.

'By the way, Jacques...' Kiely asked. 'Out of interest, which of the Joyce or Viconian cycles of history are we entering into now, do you think?'

'Chaos,' said Olivier without pause.

Fr Kiely raised his eyebrows.

You may well be right, Jacques my boy, you may well be right...Au révoir *to you and it's good morning, Shanghai.*

'God bless, Jacques,' said Fr Kiely then, and he shut the door after him.

'Amen, Father…oh, and thank you for your nice gift earlier.' 'Don't mention it. I hope you're keeping well and that your foot is good.'

'It is much improved today, Father, but the soreness comes and goes – you know.'

'Whatever happened it in the first place? You never spoke about it.'

'A little accident I had as a boy.' I winked at Fr Lee. 'Let's just say an old war wound.'

Father Lee said Mass at our little service about once a month, whenever it was safe to do so. We meet in secret and trust for the best that no-one will ever sing to the authorities. So far so good, although two other such services in our vicinity have been rumbled this year.

'Thank you for volunteering to serve Mass again. You're really good at it,' he said.

'I learned young, Father.'

'How so? You couldn't have grown up with Christianity in your youth?'

'A long story, Father. Someday I'll tell you. I might even write it all down.'

Father Lee laughed. 'Another war story, eh?'

My turn to leave, I walked up the concrete steps of the basement and into the daylight of the city, just as I had on the morning the sampan landed near Shanghai after I fled the village that last night. I looked around me for any signs of being observed, straightened up, and walked the few blocks to my apartment. I walked along the street amongst the crowds, safety in numbers I believe, staring directly ahead and not at the electronic cameras mounted on the street-lighting poles on the sidewalk. Noise comes from every angle – alarms, traffic, public announcements. I walked the hundred metres to cross the street at a busy junction, never looking behind me to see if I was followed. While waiting for the lights to turn green, I noticed a police vehicle slowly pass, and inside, observing eyes. I looked at the pavement rather than into the car.

I have noticed much more vehicles on the street now than the bicycles and rickshaws for which we are famous. Progress has certainly taken place; I have witnessed much history and heard much more, but I never after inquired of or spoke of Zhaoui. I did not wish to attract attention even though I did nothing wrong then but I did not want my memories jogged and upset by those events of long ago.

Airplane tracks in the blue sky above and the sounds around me, skyscrapers which mushroom weekly now tell a different China, yes, a different world.

I live a simple life now. I have witnessed from the sidelines the great changes in our country since those days in Zhaoui, which were themselves, historic as well as tragic. I never again desired to stand out, stand up, and be counted so to speak, although the faith Père Olivier imparted in me remains still. I often pray for him...and for Li. But not even my family knows about any of this. Knowledge can be dangerous, or perhaps it's just my age talking.

I never again heard about Johnny or Zhang, or even Zhu, who I should have liked to correspond with. Whether they survived or perished in the intervening famines or Great Leap Forwards, or not I cannot tell. Similarly whether Tang achieved greater glory or survived our Cultural Revolution – many of his sort did not. Political more than military he was, behind it all. He did in his way play his part in our history and the China of today would not be without his type. I have often considered what Tang and Père Olivier debated. Both wanted justice. One wanted it now and had faith in humanity, the other did, too, I believe, but was too pessimistic – original sin, he said – and trusted in a God and a just after-life. But yes, they both sought justice; a just world for people but in different ways and from differing perspectives. Both sought to change humanity for better according to their personal belief systems – Tang appealed to peoples' rational nature, Père Olivier to a faith – but this world has a habit of resisting being better and human nature doesn't always follow good; call us the product of millennia of surviving in a capitalistic profit-motive paradigm as Tang believed, or simply the 'original sin' of Père Olivier, our nature is base, it seems to me. These 'better' worlds of theirs still await us.

I was reluctant to tell my story. But it has been therapeutic to do so; a weight lifted – a lifetime's weight.

Another war story, said Father Lee? Well, perhaps so. That *was* war; our war. It happened to us a long time ago when men still believed in causes and nations to fight for, to kill for. For others it still happens – all the time; Jesus, Marx, Mao, Confucius, even Lao Tzu – whatever – all these names people name, worship, quote from, or simply follow.

We meet many people, and sometimes lovers, too, in our lifetime, but there is nothing like the shared experiences of childhood to make us understand and even love these friends forever. Those I remember I do with great fondness and affection. Those friends of my formative years in that place named Zhaoui, a place I do not know that even now still exists.

I am old now. But there are times, whenever I see the face of a lost dog, or gaze upon a full river in summer, or smell the budding flowers in June, I am a boy again, a bamboo stick in my hand, with Zhu by my side and my dog Misha running on ahead of us. Yes, just a hungry boy I suppose, hurrying home to his sister for supper. Just a weary traveller in search of bread.

End

结束

Jiéshù

POST-SCRIPT

The People's Republic of China was formally proclaimed by Mao Zedong, the Chairman of the Chinese Communist Party (CCP), on October 1st 1949, at three p.m. in Tiananmen Square in Peking, now Beijing, the new capital of China.

The Chinese Civil War was fought between the Kuomintang-led government of the Republic of China and forces of the Chinese Communist Party (The Red Army becoming the Peoples' Liberation Army from 1945), armed conflict continuing intermittently from 1st August 1927 until 7th December 1949, and ending with Communist control of mainland China with the Nationalists or Kuomintang under Chiang Kai-shek retreating to the island of Taiwan (formerly Formosa) which they still occupy.